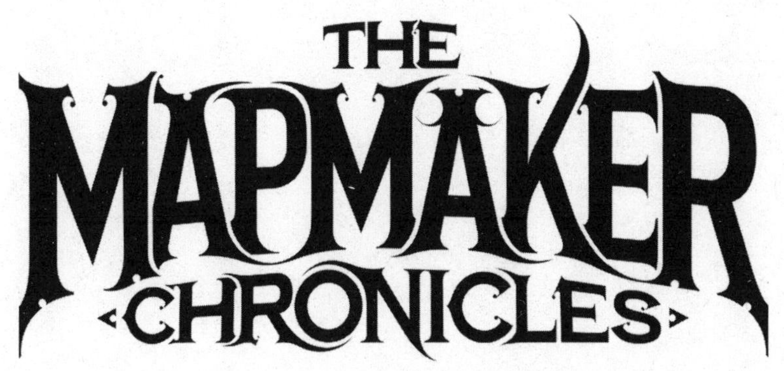

RACE TO THE END OF THE WORLD

A. L. TAIT

First American Edition 2017
Kane Miller, A Division of EDC Publishing

First published in Australia and New Zealand in 2014 by Hachette Australia (an imprint of Hachette Australia Pty Limited), this North American edition is published by arrangement with Hachette Australia Pty Ltd.

For information contact:
Kane Miller, A Division of EDC Publishing
5402 S. 122nd E. Ave, Tulsa, OK 74146
www.kanemiller.com
www.usbornebooksandmore.com

Library of Congress Control Number: 2016955642

Printed and bound in the United States of America
10 11 12 13 14 15 16 17 18 19

ISBN: 978-1-61067-622-9

For Joseph and Lucas,
who show me the world through new eyes

Prologue

His father was sending him away.

Quinn Freeman backed away from the door, stepping carefully to avoid the squeaky floorboard near the stairs. His mam always told him that listeners heard no good of themselves, and maybe she was right.

When he'd spied Master Blau at the door of their cottage earlier, with that huge Deslonder behind him, Quinn had been curious enough to leave his cozy hiding spot in the corner of the hay barn to creep inside. Now he wished he'd stayed there, tucked up with his book and his thoughts. His father had never found him there before . . .

Was it too late to hide now?

"Quinn!" he heard his father call from the other side of the door. "Quinn!"

Silence. Quinn hardly dared to breathe. He was supposed to be out in the chicken coop, clearing out the mucky hay and freshening the water.

"Quinn!" his father shouted again, rising impatience evident in the roar at the end of Quinn's name. "Blast it, where is that boy?"

Soft murmuring inside suggested his mam was answering.

Quinn froze. What to do? If he went inside, his fate was sealed. If he stayed out here, his fate was sealed. If he hid . . .

The wooden door slammed open, ricocheting against the whitewashed wall with force. "Quinn!" his brother Jed bellowed, before spotting Quinn cowering by the stairwell. "Oh, there you are," he said in his normal tone, which was about one stage lower than a bellow. "Come here!"

He reached out and grabbed Quinn by the ear. Jed was the oldest of Quinn's five brothers, who were all older than him and never let an opportunity to remind him of that fact go by. Most of those opportunities involved some form of physical punishment because, besides being older, Quinn's brothers were all bigger than he was. Much, much bigger. Even Allyn, who was only eighteen months older.

"The runt of the litter," his father called him.

"The baby," his mother called him.

Quinn wasn't sure which was worse.

"Father wants a word with you," said Jed, continuing to drag Quinn through the door by his ear and delivering him to their father's seat by the fire. The best seat in the house. The only seat with any kind of cushioning. Quinn's seat was a stool over in the farthest reaches of the large, low-ceilinged room. He didn't mind. It was quieter in the corner.

And now, with special guests, the room was full of noise. All his brothers were there – even with plowing needing to be done. As usual, they were all talking at once. The only stillness in the room was his mother, sitting beside her husband, eyes on the floor.

"Master Blau is going to take you with him," his father announced over the top of the hubbub, looking Quinn up and down. "He's looking for boys for a – what is it again?" The huge farmer turned to look at the stooped, wrinkled man currently perched on the edge of Quinn's mother's seat. The second-best seat in the house. The Deslonder stood behind him, watching.

"Hello, Quinn," said the soft-spoken old man. "I've heard a lot about you."

Quinn raised his eyebrows. Nobody talked *about* him, not ever. Well, not unless they were teasing him.

"Oh," he managed.

"The King has asked me to find ten boys for a special school," the old man continued. "I believe you are to be one of my boys."

A school? Quinn was really confused now. Farmer's sons didn't go to school. Not in Verdania. Not even the sons of freehold farmers, like his father. School was for the nobility. The rich. As his father told him every day, boys like him were born to work on farms. Like their fathers before them.

The only reason Quinn could read was because of his mother. She'd had schooling as a girl, long before she'd met and married Beyard Freeman. When her father had been at court. Before he'd been stripped of his titles and his lands.

Not that they talked about that.

But she had taught Quinn to read. The only one of the six boys. By the time Quinn had come along, his father had five sons to help around the farm. Something had happened when Quinn was born, and his mother couldn't have more babies. This meant she'd never have a daughter, so his father had "given" Quinn to his mother – to keep her company, from what he could gather.

Because of that, Quinn could cook. He could darn a sock. And he could read.

The reading thing was the trade-off for all the teasing that Quinn copped from his brothers and the other boys in the village for being a "mammy's boy." He hated that. But he loved books, and his mam had a deal with the local cleric to keep him supplied. She baked bread and made jam for the cleric, and he sent Quinn two new books a month. Precious books.

His mam had warned him that if anything ever happened to one of those books they'd all be evicted from their farm, freehold or not. Because it would cost that much to replace it. So he took great care of every volume, hiding them from his brothers, who simply didn't understand their value.

"At this stage, it's just for three months," Master Blau said, frail voice cracking. "But if you do well, much longer."

"If you do well, you'll get to go off on adventures!" interrupted Jed. At twenty-one, Jed didn't always see eye to eye with their father. Quinn knew Jed was keen for a few adventures of his own, but their father had made it quite clear that Jed's place was on the farm.

Quinn frowned. He didn't like the sound of adventures. At fourteen, he did not share Jed's desire to leave Markham. Not at all. He wanted to stay here, with his family and his books. He loved the little cottage with its whitewashed walls and thatched roof. His brothers drove him mad, but they were also great fun when they wanted to be. And he always felt safe with them. Nobody messed with the Freeman boys.

"Now, now, let's not put the cart before the horse," said his father. "Only three boys will do that. And he'll be competing with nobility and all."

Quinn's frown deepened. What the blazes was going on? He turned to look at his mam, eyes searching her face for answers. She looked tired and drawn, and wouldn't quite meet his gaze.

"Allow me to explain," said Master Blau. "King Orel has called upon me to find the ten most promising students in the land to train as mapmakers. He has decided that Verdania will create the first map of the world."

Map of the world? Why did he want one of those? Besides, everyone knew that if you went too far in either direction, you'd fall off the end of the earth. They also knew that below the drop lay Genesi, dragon of death, waiting. Quinn had spent his whole life hearing stories of Genesi.

"Why would he want that?" asked Allyn. "It's not much bigger than Athelstan, Gelyn and Firenze, is it?"

Quinn saw the big Deslonder wince at the comment. Quinn wasn't entirely sure where Deslond was, but he knew it was somewhere well beyond the boundaries of Firenze. People still talked about the time the men of the village had gone to fight in the Crusadic Wars, twenty years earlier, and had been gone the better part of five years.

Five years suggested there was a bit of travel involved.

"The King has heard that Gelyn is planning to develop such a map," said Master Blau, in the casual tone reserved for those who dealt with matters of state all the time. "The King does not wish Gelyn to have more knowledge than we do."

Quinn could understand that. It hadn't taken him long to work out that knowledge meant power. His brothers might be physically stronger than he was, but he knew more about history and seasons and . . . well, just about everything than they did. They could only know what they saw, or heard. He could read the thoughts of scholars and clerics and prophets and storytellers. Given time, he could know everything.

"Why me?" Quinn asked. The first words he'd spoken since he'd been dragged into the room.

"Cleric Redland told us about you," said Master Blau. "We have been in contact with every cleric and tutor and master in the kingdom, looking for the right boys for our . . . project."

Once again, Quinn turned towards his mother. He'd only met Cleric Redland a few times. Mostly his mother took care of book deliveries and drop-offs. What could Cleric Redland possibly know about him that meant he'd be dragged into this?

"He knows about your memory," she said, quietly. "I told him."

Quinn blanched. He'd been only four when his family had realized that he had a strange quirk. They'd been sitting around the long wooden table in the kitchen as his mother had served up a particularly delicious stew of lamb and potatoes. His father, a man who usually focused on his food, had been feeling sentimental that night and had asked his wife if she remembered the "dinner poem," as he called it. She'd laughed.

"I haven't recited that in years," she said. "I don't think I'd even remember where to start."

And, sitting on his stool at the bottom of the table, Quinn had calmly begun to speak:

"Where, oh where, is my dinner, cried the little snake.
I know I left it here somewhere; I slept, now I'm awake.
I've looked all over, up and down, everywhere I've tried.
Oh wait, I think I've found it here . . . Tucked up in my insides.
Oh where, oh where is my dinner, cried the little –"

He'd gotten no further than that before the room erupted. It was a poem he'd heard only once, at least two years before. After that, it hadn't taken them long to realize that Quinn remembered everything. *Everything.* From what they'd had for dinner on any given night six months before, to every single word he read. He could describe in detail the contents of each peddler's cart that regularly visited the farm, and when they were last there, so that his mother could work out how best to spend her money. And he knew, by heart, every recipe she'd ever made.

When he'd gotten older, his father had asked him how he did it. As best he could explain, it was as though he had a stack of pictures in his mind and he simply flicked through them until he found the one with the information he wanted.

His family was used to it now, but they were careful to keep the secret of Quinn's memory from the rest of the village. Quinn knew that not everyone would be as understanding of something that couldn't be explained. He'd never forget the sight of his friend Aysha's mother being hounded out of the village by a group of angry, masked villagers because she couldn't explain why her plant remedies cured illness when doctors couldn't. Despite her pleas, despite the fact that the villagers had known her for years – nothing she'd said could convince them that she was no witch, no threat. And so Sarina, Aysha's mother, had left, weeping, under a hail of sticks and stones.

Quinn had run as fast as he could to get his own mother, but they hadn't seen Sarina – or Aysha – since.

And now here was this old man, discussing his memory like it was an everyday thing.

"Your mother says you can read, and write," Master Blau was saying. "I think you have the makings of a fine candidate for the project."

"I don't want to go," said Quinn, flatly. "I want to stay here."

His mother started sobbing.

"You don't get to choose," his father told him, no expression in the hazel eyes that were so similar to Quinn's own. "*We* don't get to choose. Master Blau has chosen you and that's that."

Master Blau laughed softly. "Well, there's no need to be dramatic about it," he said, before turning to look directly at Quinn. "The fact is that it takes a special person to create maps. There are very few candidates available and the King is most, er, adamant that I get this program underway as soon as possible. Besides . . ." He paused, looking around the humble living room of the cottage intently.

Quinn tried to see it through his eyes. One long, low room with heavy, dark wooden beams across the ceiling. Flagstone flooring. Simple wooden furniture. A large open hearth at one end. It wasn't much to look at, he realized. But it was home.

"Each boy who is chosen to undertake the journey will be paid," Master Blau was saying, "a stipend of twenty deckerts a month while he is away, a bonus of five hundred deckerts on his return, and the granting of a parcel of land should his ship prove to be the winner."

Quinn's mouth dropped open. Twenty deckerts was more than his father made in a year. The rest constituted riches beyond his imagination. He could see why his father was so keen for him to go. With six sons and a small land holding, Beyard Freeman was going to struggle to find work for them all. With all that money and extra land . . . well, the sky was the limit.

Quinn stole a quick glance at his brothers. Jed was looking at him with open envy, Simon with longing – Quinn knew that he had his eye on the blacksmith's daughter, Merryn, and he knew that Simon had no chance whatsoever in his current state as second son of a farmer. The others, Heath, Berrick and Allyn, simply looked bemused. He knew they'd never imagined a time *ever* that it would be he, Quinn, who held the family's fortunes in his hands.

"So you see, Quinn," his father said, "there's really no choice. You must go to Master Blau's school and you must do your best."

Quinn sighed as he stared at the floor. He couldn't argue with his father – he wanted the best for his family, too.

Besides, there'd be competition, wouldn't there?

"Who else is going?" he asked, raising his eyes and addressing Master Blau directly for the first time.

"Most of the others are sons of noblemen," the old man said. "One is a cleric's fosterling. And you."

Quinn exhaled with relief. It would all work out because, frankly, he had no chance to be chosen as one of the three scribes! He'd heard that the children of nobility were schooled in everything from languages to swordplay every day from the age of eight. He couldn't imagine such luxury. Surely his mother's sporadic reading and writing lessons couldn't compete with that. "What happens to those who are not chosen?" he asked.

If he had to go away, Quinn hoped it would benefit his family in some way, even if it was a waste of time.

Master Blau laughed. "Ten deckerts a month for three months for each boy who attends the school," he said.

More than a year's farm income. It would help a great deal, given the season they were having. The previous winter had been hard and the spring hadn't brought its usual heavy rains. It was now the beginning of summer and the crops were struggling and Quinn had heard his father and Jed talking long into the night about what they were going to do.

He looked at his mother. She had stopped crying. She knew as well as he did what he needed to do – but he needed her support to do it. She nodded, before giving him one of her slow, sweet smiles.

"You'll be chosen," she told him.

Everyone laughed. "There you are," his father said. "Your mam's never wrong, so you might as well pack your bag."

Quinn managed a smile. His father was right. There was no choice in this, not for him. His family needed him to go and to do his best. He was the only one of them who could do it, so do it he must.

As far as being chosen, though – well, he couldn't be as sure of that as his mam was. And he couldn't help but hope she was wrong. Just this once.

In the meantime, though, he might as well try to enjoy the fact that he'd be doing exactly what he loved for three months. Reading. Writing. Learning.

How bad could it be?

Chapter One

Three months later

If Quinn had had a worse day, he couldn't remember it. And given that he remembered everything, he was pretty sure that meant this was the worst day. Ever.

It had begun that morning before the sun had even thought about lighting the sky, had continued through a long day of pushing, shoving and snide remarks, and here he was in the dark, with the moon full and the Mid Hour almost upon him, and it was still unfolding. Worst of all, it all came down to one thing – or one person, rather.

Ira.

From his first day at scribe school, as the King had deemed it, Ira had decided that Quinn didn't belong. The fact that Ira was probably right didn't make it any easier when he'd decided to make Quinn's life a living nightmare to prove his point. The tall, blond boy took every chance to make Quinn look bad. And there were many chances.

Given his position as the son of a Lordling, Ira should really have had better things to do with his time. All the other noble boys in the group went out of their way to ignore Quinn, to the point where they would simply walk over the top of him if he got in their way.

But not Ira. He'd made it clear from day one that he was personally affronted by the fact that a farmer's son had been selected for the school. The fact that Quinn had proved himself more than capable of keeping up in class (which had surprised nobody more than Quinn himself) had only added to the problem.

Ira, with his fancy leather breeches and his soft, fine-weave tunics, poked fun at Quinn's coarse, homespun clothing. He had only two sets, while Ira seemed to have new clothes to wear every day. Quinn didn't mind that – he could picture his mam weaving the cloth for his simple tunic, then sewing it by hand, each stitch tinier than the next. He'd sewn part of his breeches himself – not that he'd be sharing that information with Ira. His mam had shown him how to turn the seams and how to create the little loops with which the breeches were fastened.

Unfortunately, he was now wondering if he'd ever see those breeches again.

At present he was sitting, shivering, in the dark in two inches of cold, grimy water. His breeches, which he'd set next to the bath when he'd climbed in half an hour before, were somewhere else in the castle. Ira and his gang had snuck into the tower washroom and stolen all Quinn's clothes as he had his weekly bath, which he only took at this late hour in an attempt to avoid them. So much for that. They hadn't even left him with a drying cloth, and had blown out all the candles and locked the door on the way out, leaving Quinn alone and naked in the dark. He'd sat there, stunned, while valuable minutes ticked by. If there was one thing Quinn hated, it was the dark.

Even if he could work out how to break down the solid wooden door, he would need to navigate the narrow, circular stone staircase that led down to the dormitory wing where he and his fellow students lived. And he certainly wasn't going to do that naked.

Gingerly he stood, feeling the cool water run down his legs and drip into the tub. He could just about see his hand in front of his face if he held it at the very end of his nose. Feeling for the lip of the tub, he lifted one leg out onto the cold stone floor. It was slippery under his wet feet, but now that he was out of the high tub, he could see a line of light leaking in under the door.

He immediately felt better. There had been no light before. Quinn had been enjoying his late bath – a luxury for a boy who'd shared a washtub full of water once a week with the seven other members of his family – trying to calm his nerves for the next day: Decision Day. All the lights in the other dormitory rooms had been out as he'd climbed the stairs, and he'd assumed everyone else was asleep. Clearly, he'd been wrong where Ira was concerned. He could only hope that the light he could now see was not Ira, waiting at the bottom of the stairs for Quinn to try to escape.

He moved towards the door and hammered on it.

"Help!" he said. "Help!"

He paused, listening hard to see if anyone was coming. Were those footsteps on the stairs?

He hammered again. Stopped. Heard the shuffle of feet outside the door.

"Is someone in there?" a voice whispered.

Quinn breathed a sigh of relief. Ajax. The cleric's fosterling was a large, friendly boy with a huge, contagious smile. Ira and his gang left Ajax alone, mostly, Quinn thought, because the size of him terrified them. He reminded Quinn of his brothers: the same knockabout manner and the same interests – games, girls and doing as little work as possible. Quinn had initially wondered how Ajax had found himself in the group of ten students. He didn't seem the studious type and he didn't have the benefit of background that Ira and his gang had.

What Ajax did have, Quinn had learned over time, was an ability to turn his hands to any practical task and the constitution of an ox. Ajax wasn't the quickest student at the school either physically or mentally, but he was unfailingly good-natured and he had a surprising talent for drawing, adding quirky little touches to his work. Add to that his red hair – which everyone knew was a good-luck omen – and Quinn thought Ajax was pretty much a shoo-in to be chosen for the Great Race, as it had come to be known.

Great Race. Even the words had the ability to make Quinn shudder. Mind you, it could simply be cold that was making him shiver violently now.

"It's me," he whispered, "Quinn. I'm stuck in here."

"Oh," said the big redhead. "I see. Someone's locked the door! Who would do such a thing?" He sounded genuinely outraged. If there was one thing Ajax hated, it was unfairness.

"It doesn't matter," Quinn said now, knowing that the last thing he needed tonight was to escalate his troubles with Ira. "But can you let me out?"

"Of course," said Ajax, and Quinn could hear him turning the key in the lock. "Just give me a sec – it's a bit stiff."

"Er, one thing," Quinn said, as Ajax continued to rattle the key. "I'm going to need something to put on."

"You're what?" Ajax said, obviously concentrating hard on the task at hand.

"I've got no clothes," Quinn said, louder. "You'll have to get me something to wear."

As he said the last words, Ajax finally got the key to work, flung the door open and rushed into the room – right into Quinn, sending him flying backward.

There was nothing like having your naked buttocks hit cold stone at speed to really top off a terrible day, thought Quinn as he sat, splayed on the floor, blinking up at Ajax as the light hit his eyes.

"Oh, gosh, sorry," the redhead said. "Oh, but wait, you're nude! Here!" With that he peeled off the nightshirt he was wearing, leaving him in an undershirt and drawers.

Quinn stood slowly, took the shirt and dropped it over his head, where it swallowed his entire body, right down to his ankles.

"Thanks, Ajax," he muttered. "I'll just go and change and bring you back your shirt."

"Before you go, let me show you a trick," the larger boy offered.

Quinn eyed him warily. He was cold, tired and facing another long, trying day in a matter of hours. Now was possibly not the best time for a trick of any description. But Ajax had been helpful . . .

"Before I went to live with Cleric Fennelly, I was in an orphanage," he was saying, as chatty as though the two of them were sitting in one of Queen Lorelei's parlors, drinking honeyed tea. "The Guardians used to lock us in our rooms all the time. So we learned how to get out of them. Let me show you."

With that, he turned back to the door. "I'll show you and then I'll lock the door and you can try it," he said. "The trick is to try to open the door from the other side. It's not as easy when you're naked, of course, but most of the time you'll have something in your pocket that will help. Let me just have a look around here and see if I can find – aha!"

He had been crawling about on the floor, feeling with his fingers, and now stood triumphantly with a thin sliver of one of the floor stones in his hand. He turned to the door and, rather than going to the handle, approached the other side.

"What you want to do is to remove the hinges," he was saying, demonstrating for Quinn how to use the thin sliver of stone to turn the screws in the hinges. "That way, you don't draw attention to yourself, and rather than wasting energy trying to shove at a door that won't move, you simply open it from the other side."

Quinn watched in fascination as the hinges came free and Ajax was able to pry the door open from the wrong side.

"Right," said Ajax, turning to Quinn. "Your turn." With that, he screwed the hinges back on, attaching them once more, and then went through the door. Quinn set to work on the hinges with the little rock that Ajax had given him and within minutes felt the hinges come free. He opened the door to Ajax's hundred-deckert grin.

"Well done!" the larger boy said, clapping Quinn across the back and knocking the breath out of him. "Now you've done it once, you'll never forget it."

Quinn stilled. No one at the school had any idea about his memory and Master Blau had told him on the way to the school three months earlier to keep it a secret. Not that Quinn needed telling. He could just imagine the response of Ira and the others if his freakish feats were revealed. So he'd made sure he'd asked questions in class, even when he knew the answers because he'd read them or been told them before. Had he somehow given himself away? But Ajax looked at him with complete innocence.

It was just an expression.

He smiled back at Ajax, who took the stone and quickly screwed the door hinges back into position. "Never leave them loose," he told Quinn. "You don't want to give away your secrets . . ."

Quinn laughed for the first time in months. "No," he agreed. "It wouldn't be right to do that!"

"Okay then, we'd best get to bed," said Ajax. "Big day tomorrow."

Decision Day. Tomorrow the three explorers selected by King Orel to compete for the honor of mapping the world would choose their scribes. Armed with compasses, rulers, precious vellum, ink and all the knowledge that Master Blau had been able to cram into their heads in three months, the boys would undertake the task of creating beautiful, precise records of the world around them.

They weren't starting from scratch, of course. Verdania had a healthy tradition of mapmaking, and mapmakers like Master Blau had created a series of detailed maps of the kingdom and those around it, such as Firenze and Gelyn. Quinn had even seen a hasty map drawn by one of the brave soldiers from the Crusadic Wars, which showed the path they had taken to Deslond. He'd been surprised to see that the soldier, Dolan, had allocated spaces to other kingdoms along the way. At the time, nobody had stopped to do any exploring so there were no details about what those kingdoms were, nor who lived there, but the soldier had taken care to mark the rivers and mountains they'd passed, and had detailed a small section of coastline.

Was that the beginning of the end of the earth?

Quinn hoped he never had to find out. The more he learned about mapmaking, the more he'd realized it wasn't for him. Although one side of him loved it. He took great pride in his maps, drawing each detail with care and adding illustrations where he thought they would make things clearer. He'd often seen Master Blau looking approvingly at his work.

But it was one thing to create beautiful maps and quite another thing to realize what those maps represented, for all the maps Quinn had seen had ended. The land gave way to vast swathes of blue water – just how big, no one knew. But Quinn had seen enough to know that the direction of travel for this expedition was all wrong. The direction of the ocean currents and the winds was wrong, aiming to push any ship *backward*, meaning any progress would be slow and dangerous. As well, sailors who had ventured out beyond the boundaries of current maps reported vicious storms and ferocious oceans. Frankly, he couldn't see how any expedition would last beyond a week.

On top of that, while Master Blau had spent countless hours discussing with him and the class the latest theories about why the earth was round, Quinn wasn't entirely sure he believed it.

If the earth was round, just how did all that water stay in place? And if the earth was round, just where was it? He would lie on his back in the palace gardens staring up at the sky. The sky was up. The earth was down. If you dug a hole, you went farther down – to Hell, the clerics said.

If the earth was round, that meant that somewhere, the sky was below him. And that if you dug a hole and kept going, you'd eventually get to the other side.

Seriously, it made his brain hurt just to think about it.

And it made him want to take his thirty deckerts and go home to the farm where nobody talked about the possibility of sailing off the end of the earth.

"Do you want to be chosen?" he asked Ajax. He hadn't had this conversation with anyone since he'd been at the school. With some, you didn't need to. Ira and his gang were convinced they were going to be chosen. Ira was constantly telling everyone what a great kick start to his knight's career the whole exercise was going to be. He'd made it clear from day one that he was simply filling in time before he could become a squire at sixteen.

There were others who you could tell were simply not going to be chosen. Like Anders, a shy, pimply boy of thirteen who slept with a small felt doll every night and who'd been ill three times since his arrival at the school. He was incredibly bright, with a great knowledge of the stars, but Quinn couldn't see how he'd even leave the harbor without needing a doctor.

Master Blau had told them all that the explorers were looking for a combination of skills, health and tenacity in their scribes. Each of them was different, he'd said, so their own opinions on the importance of those things would, of course, factor in, but Quinn would bet that none of them would take a chance on Anders.

The journey they were to undertake was a long and arduous one. King Orel's rules stated that, to win the race, the explorer had to return to Verdania with the most beautiful and detailed map within one year. Additional treasure would be looked upon favorably.

Quinn had spent some time wondering just how far you could sail in a ship in a year. No matter which way he looked at it, it was farther than he wanted to imagine.

Treasure or no treasure, to bring back a beautiful and detailed map, the explorer would also need to bring back his scribe. Losing a scribe halfway around the world was a good way to forfeit the race.

Which is why, Quinn thought, looking at the back of Ajax's large head as he followed the other boy down the stairs, Ajax was a shoo-in. He looked indestructible.

"I don't really mind one way or the other," Ajax was saying, concentrating on putting one large foot in front of the other. The stairs to the washroom were narrow and he had to turn his feet sideways to gain solid purchase on each one. "I think it would be fun, to see all those different places and find out what's out there, but . . . I would miss Cleric Fennelly and he's getting old now. I think he needs me at home, though he wouldn't say it."

Quinn knew that Ajax had been with the cleric for four years. He'd been sent from the orphanage to live with him when the cleric had fallen and broken his hip. Ajax had done his fetching and carrying and had so charmed him with his innately sunny nature that Cleric Fennelly had refused to send him back when his hip mended. And so Ajax had stayed.

"What about you?" Ajax asked.

"I don't think I've got much chance," Quinn said, evading the question as he'd evaded nearly every personal question put to him during his time at the school. He'd kept himself to himself, partly because he was so homesick, partly to keep his secret, and partly because he spent most of his free time in the palace gardens. But nobody knew about that either.

"Oh, I don't know," said Ajax lightly. "Your maps are definitely the most detailed."

It was true, Quinn acknowledged silently. Mostly because he remembered exactly what he'd seen in the other maps he'd studied.

"Yes, but I'm the smallest of the group, bar Anders," he said out loud, trying to convince himself as much as Ajax. "Even my father calls me a runt."

Ajax laughed. "My mam always said, 'Good things come in small packages,'" he said. "She died when I was five, so she didn't live to see me outgrow my 'small' phase. But I always remember her saying that."

Quinn managed a smile. "My mam says that, too," he said.

Ajax stopped on the stairs, three from the bottom. "You don't want to go, do you?" he asked. He wasn't challenging Quinn, merely interested.

Quinn took a deep breath. "Not really," he said. "I didn't even want to come here, but my family needed the money and . . ." His words trailed away.

"Don't you want to see the world?"

"Not really," Quinn said again. "I like the part of the world I know." He thought of the flat green fields that stretched out like blankets around the family's stone cottage. He thought of the wide brown river that ran through the tiny village of Markham, where he'd been born and where he knew everyone and they knew him. He loved sailing his little skiff out with the tide, down to collect shellfish at the mouth where the river met the ocean.

"Well, hopefully they'll choose someone else then," said Ajax cheerfully.

And that was the crux of the matter. Quinn had no say in whether he was chosen or not. He'd kept his promise to his father and done his best, knowing that the money he would earn for being part of the race would matter to every member of his family. But that didn't mean he had to like it.

"If you turn up in my nightshirt, you've got a pretty good chance of being left behind," Ajax continued, laughing at his own joke.

Quinn looked down at the volumes of fabric swirling at his ankles. "You're right," he answered with his own laugh. "Maybe Ira's done me a favor."

Ajax stopped laughing and looked thoughtful. "Ira took your clothes, huh?" he said. "Then come with me. I think I know where they'll be."

Quinn followed him down the hall to the scullery at the entrance to the dormitory. "Ira's been flirting with that Brianna who does the washing," Ajax said. "I bet he's stashed them in here."

Sure enough, after a bit of digging around amongst the unwashed smalls of everyone at scribe school, Quinn had his clothes back.

"Thanks, Ajax," he said as he dropped the redhead off outside his room on his own way to bed. "I really appreciate the help."

"Any time. It's a shame we didn't really speak until tonight."

"Oh well, I'll be there to wave you off tomorrow as you head out into the big world," Quinn joked.

Ajax laughed. "You'd like that, wouldn't you? Well, be careful, Quinn – it might be *me* doing the waving off."

The image of Ajax waving him off from the docks as he stood on deck bound for Who Knows Where kept Quinn awake for many hours that night.

Chapter Two

Despite a restless night, Quinn was awake before dawn – thanks to Ira. The boy had woken early, tiptoed into his room with a full jug of water, and poured it over Quinn's head as he'd done every morning that week. By the time Quinn was up and on his feet, sputtering and soaked, Ira had raced back to his own room. Quinn knew there was no point in chasing him and raising a ruckus – the blond boy would simply put on his most innocent expression and deny all knowledge.

Quinn sighed, quickly stripping his wet nightshirt and turning back his blanket to give his sheets the best possible chance to dry during the day. Not that he'd need them again that night. No matter what happened today, he wouldn't sleep in this bed again. He'd either be on a cart heading back to Markham and his family, or on a ship.

He slid into his breeches and tunic, put his few possessions into the hessian bag he'd brought with him three months earlier, picked up his worn leather boots and tiptoed down the hall to the back stairs that led from the dormitory wing, out of the castle and down into the gardens. Truth be told, he didn't mind being woken early – though he could have done without the icy bath – for it gave him a chance to slip away to the kitchen garden before breakfast.

He'd discovered the garden on his second day in the castle, when he'd blundered into it while trying to find the breakfast hall. It was a beautiful walled space, laid out in sectors around a large circular "knot" in the center. Each sector contained different vegetables, while the knot overflowed with more types of herbs than he'd ever seen. He'd been wandering about, feeling the texture of the different leaves under his fingers, breathing in the different scents released as he did so, when a voice behind him had stopped him in his tracks.

"Just what do you think you're doing?"

"Oh, I, er . . ." He turned to face the speaker, to explain, when she suddenly shrieked, ran forward and grabbed him from behind in a hard hug, squeezing the breath from his middle.

"Quinn! Oh, Quinn! What are you doing here?"

Aysha! He tried to speak, but couldn't, as she hugged him even tighter. All he could do was wave his arms about and struggle for air. She wasn't a big girl, dark-haired (like him), with blue eyes and a smattering of freckles, but she was a lot stronger than she looked.

When she finally released him, babbling nineteen to the dozen about how pleased she was to see him, he had to sit down on the low stone wall around the knot garden to catch his breath.

"What's wrong?" she demanded. "Aren't you pleased to see me?"

He managed a laugh. That was Aysha. She had always been the most forthright girl he'd ever known. They'd met in the village at the Mayfair when they were both eight, and had been friends ever since.

He frowned. "Of course I am," he said. "If a little surprised. I thought you were dead! Where have you been all this time? How did you get here? What happened to your mam?"

Her smile slid away. "She's dead, Quinn. After we ran . . . well, she got sick. I think they broke her heart. She was just devastated about what happened. We walked and walked and walked and she got weaker and weaker. We ended up here . . . I think maybe she thought she'd be safer in a big city."

She paused and sank to sit beside him, staring at her feet. He awkwardly put his arm around her.

"We'd only been here three days when she died," Aysha went on, voice rising to a wail. "She was so weak from walking and . . . so sick."

Now the tears started. Quinn started patting her shoulder, not sure what to say.

"My poor mother!" said Aysha, sniffing and wiping the tears from her face. She pulled a square of cotton from her skirt and blew her nose. "Just because those ignoramuses don't understand the healing power of herbs. To turn on her like that – like she was a witch!"

Quinn wished he knew what to say. He'd known Sarina, Aysha's mother, well. She was a kind, quiet woman, more at home with plants and flowers than she'd ever been with humans. She and Aysha had lived in a little hut, close to the forest, where they'd kept a few chickens and a large vegetable garden. The pair had lived off the money they raised selling what they didn't need.

The trouble had all started the previous winter when the local tax collector's baby son had gone down with a terrible fever. When the usual doctoring – leeches, bloodletting, compresses – had failed to cure the boy, his father had gone in desperation to Sarina's door, begging her to help him. She'd resisted at first. She knew that the village didn't look kindly on her "potions" as they called them. Her knowledge of plants and herbs had been passed down through her family and reached back to a time that the ladies of the village now called "uncivilized."

But the man had been desperate and so she'd brewed up a special blend of herbs and taken it to his house. The next day, the child, who had been at death's door, was sitting up in his basket, cooing at his mother, cheeks rosy with health. And the ladies had not liked it, branding Sarina a witch and her knowledge ungodly. After a day or two of muttering, an angry mob, armed with masks and sticks and stones, had gone to Sarina's house and driven her from the village.

And the ladies had applauded.

Quinn's mother had been furious at the whole turn of events. She had rushed back to Aysha's house as soon as Quinn fetched her. But they'd been too late. Sarina was gone and so too was Aysha. Never to be seen again. Until now.

"But why are you here?" he asked. She was wearing a dark woolen dress and stiff white apron, like he'd seen on the other servants in the castle. "You work here?"

"Yes," she said. "After my mother died, I had no money and I couldn't think of anywhere else to go, so I came to the castle. Luckily, one of the guards at the gate felt sorry for me and brought me here to work with his wife. I had nothing to go back to Markham for, Quinn. I'm sorry."

Quinn nodded, troubled. He hated to think of her going through all of that by herself.

"Are you okay here?" he asked.

"As okay as I can be," she said. "I have somewhere to live, food to eat, and I get to work with plants every day . . ."

He could hear the ache for her mother in her voice.

"But what about you?" she said. "Why are you here?"

He explained about the school and the race. Her eyes widened with every word.

"Oh, Quinn, you're so lucky," she breathed. "I'd love to go away like that. Imagine what you might find out there."

He couldn't tell her then that he didn't want to go. She'd always been so brave and adventurous and when he was with her, he was the same. She'd say, "Let's take the skiff out into the harbor and see what's there," and he'd agree. If he were on his own, he'd only go to the mouth of the river and enjoy the view. With Aysha, there was no question of just looking – you had to get into the picture.

So he'd nodded, and they'd spent time together, catching up, before the breakfast bell had rung and they'd gone their separate ways. Since then, they'd met every morning, talking about everything from the plants in the garden to the people in his class. And this morning would be their last.

He sat on the low stone wall and breathed deeply. The sun was just reaching the garden and the herbs were waking up for the day, releasing their scent in the crisp morning breeze. He could smell the soft perfume of the lavender, the pungent scent of the rosemary, the fresh tang of mint. Absentmindedly, he rubbed a sage leaf between his fingers, enjoying the fuzzy feeling on his skin.

There was no sign of Aysha yet. He yawned and frowned. Where could she be? She knew that today was the last chance they'd have to speak for a long time. Whether he went to sea, where she wouldn't be able to visit him, or went home to the farm, where she would, but not until the feast of Stephen, it would be at least six months before their next conversation.

He watched the sun rise over the wall, feeling its gentle heat through his shirt. The days were definitely getting cooler, but he loved autumn, with its bright-blue skies and clear mornings.

Lost in thought, he didn't realize the passage of time until the breakfast bell sounded. Startled, he sat up and looked around. He'd been sitting here for over an hour and Aysha hadn't come. Something must have happened to her!

He tore over to the back door of the kitchen, asking the scullery maid, who was emptying a large pot of something unidentifiable into the pig trough, if she had seen Aysha that morning. She hadn't. Neither had the footman, the stable boy, the cook, nor any of the other dozen people he asked on his way to breakfast.

It was as though she'd vanished.

Quinn ate a hurried breakfast of oats and honey, washed down with cold tea, before running out the door to begin his search again. Unfortunately, he ran directly into the chest of Master Blau.

"Ah, Quinn, I've been looking for you," the old man

said. "It's time. The King requests your presence in the Counting House for the Decision."

Quinn gulped. In his mad search for Aysha, he'd nearly managed to forget what day it was. And he knew that "requests your presence" was Master Blau's polite way of saying "orders your presence – right now." Master Blau was accompanied, as always, by the huge Deslonder. Quinn had learned that he was the King's personal slave, captured twenty years earlier in the Crusadic Wars. In the ensuing years, the dark-skinned man had been a constant presence by the King's side. Whispers had it that they conducted themselves more as friends than as master/slave when not in public.

Now the man – named Zain – was staring at Quinn, as though he could see right through his skin and into his heart. Quinn shivered. With his scarred face and gold earrings, Zain was unlike anyone Quinn had ever known. Perhaps he *could* see right through people.

"Just on my way," he stammered now, in response to Master Blau's statement. Aysha would have to wait until after the Decision. With any luck he'd have five minutes to find her before he was dispatched back to the village.

"Excellent," said Master Blau. "We'll accompany you there. Just to make sure you don't get lost."

Quinn shot him a quick look. Master Blau knew of Quinn's reticence to attend scribe school, of course – he'd been there for the conversation with Quinn's family. But

Quinn had been careful not to show anything of the sort during his time here. He had done everything asked of him – and more – to ensure that the precious deckerts he'd been promised would make it home to his family. All his wishful thinking about not being chosen had been just that – *thinking*.

Perhaps the Deslonder was not the only one who could see inside a person's skin.

But the old mapmaker was looking serenely ahead, apparently unaware of the internal turmoil in the boy alongside him.

Quinn breathed a sigh of relief. All he had to do was maintain the act for another few hours and he'd be free.

There was no way he'd be chosen. No sane explorer would choose the smallest – bar one – of the ten candidates.

Chapter Three

King Orel stared down at the three men standing before him. The Chosen Three. It would be they who would bring him his precious map of the world – or die trying. Ever since he'd heard from his spies in the Gelynion court that his mortal enemy, Rey Bernadino, had his hands on a rudimentary map that suggested the world was round, he'd wanted to go one better.

At this stage, he knew, the map was merely the guesswork of famed Gelynion explorer Mendello Dorado, but the ruler who managed to prove him right – or wrong – would hold untold power. Not only would he have potential access to new lands and the treasures they might hold, but he would have knowledge of the fastest, safest shipping routes.

The possibilities – for expansion, for wealth – were unlimited.

And anything Gelyn could do, Verdania could do better.

He frowned, considering the men before him. When he'd first announced his desire to secure a map of the world, he'd offered no prize. He wanted to see who might come forward merely for the glory. Only one man had done so, and he was standing on the far left of the line of bowed heads.

John Dolan, an explorer of some repute, looked stiff with tension. King Orel knew that he was keen to get started – had wanted to set out four months ago, in fact. When he'd heard he had to wait for a scribe to be trained, he hadn't been happy. But, as King Orel pointed out, there wasn't much point in setting out to create a map without a mapmaker on board.

On paper, Dolan, who went by one name to most of Verdania, was a clear favorite for the race, and King Orel knew for a fact that the money changers in the back alleys were taking bets on Dolan returning first. King Orel was not so sure. Every time he spoke with Dolan, he became less and less certain of the man's abilities. Yes, he'd performed creditably in the Crusadic Wars and had managed to draft out a scrappy mud map of the progress of the army through neighboring countries, but the songs sung about him were now at least twenty years old. The Great Explorer, it seemed, had been content to explore only his backyard for the past two decades.

Given those misgivings, he had decided to open things up by offering a reward. And it was quite a reward. The explorer who returned with the clearest and most beautiful map would win the prize of his choice. Dolan had chosen gold. Gold and glory. Which, given the man's previous occupation as a soldier for hire, was probably to be expected.

The man standing next in line was quite a different proposition. Odilon of Blenheim looked ill at ease in his silk stockings, slippers and embossed velvet tunic. As well he might. Standing between two men dressed in worn leather breeches, simple hemp shirts and scuffed knee-high boots, he looked as out of place as a fish on a jetty. When he'd first presented as a candidate for the race, King Orel had looked at him askance. Why would this perfumed popinjay, particularly one so popular with the ladies, want to put himself through such danger and hardship?

The answer had arrived soon enough. Odilon wanted power. His choice of prize, should he win, was a seat on the King's own council. A prize indeed for a minor Lord like himself, and not something he could ever hope to win without the race. Discreet investigations into Odilon's finances showed that he could afford to buy himself the best and most comfortable ship, an experienced crew and every assistance he could wish for to give him the best possible chance in the race.

King Orel had granted him permission to compete.

And then here was the third man. King Orel's eyes drifted upward. Even with his head bowed, this man required respect, a fact the King had discovered during the twenty years in which Zain had been his personal slave. When Zain had asked permission to compete, King Orel's first instinct had been to say no. Not only because he had saved the King's life on more than one occasion, but because he had proved himself a fine, intelligent sounding board over the years they had been together. Quite simply, this man who had been his captive was now his friend.

Queen Lorelei had convinced him, however, that Zain deserved a chance. He wanted only one thing: his freedom. King Orel was torn between wanting him to win for his friend's sake, and wanting him to lose for his own.

Of course, for appearances, he had made it clear that Zain would have company on his quest. Firstly, Cleric Greenfield would travel on his ship to ensure Zain did not simply sail off into the sunset the minute he left the harbor. Not that Cleric Greenfield would be able to stop him if Zain chose to do just that, King Orel acknowledged, looking at the size difference between the shaggy cleric in his long brown wool tunic and the mountainous slave. As extra insurance, Zain's wife and daughter would remain in the castle, under watch at all times. The King knew that the big man would never leave Verdania without his family.

The other two explorers were standing as far from Zain as possible, King Orel noted with an inward smile. They had been horrified when he'd told them who the third man would be, bleating on about the fact that they could never compete with a man who was "not like" them. A man owned by another.

He had closed his ears, and had shut the men up with one wave of his hand, pointing out that they should be pleased. If Zain were indeed as inferior as they claimed, it would make the odds better for the two of them. They'd looked at each other, then back at him and nodded, and the King had heard no more from them.

Not that the rest of the court wasn't whispering about it. He'd kept the news under wraps until the very last minute, announcing it to his inner circle only that morning over breakfast. But the news had spread like wildfire. In fact, he was willing to bet that the only people who *didn't* know who the three explorers were, were the ten boys now waiting in the antechamber outside his Counting Room. He'd had Master Blau round them up immediately after breakfast. They'd been cooling their heels for around two hours, so he figured the time was probably right to bring them in.

"You will soon choose your scribes," he announced to the explorers waiting at the foot of his throne. "I know that Master Blau has provided you with ample information about each of the boys – age, background, strengths, weaknesses, and so on and so forth. I also know that you have been given the opportunity to observe the boys from afar during their morning exercise class to help you judge their physical prowess. Now I shall bring them in, one by one, and we shall hear your judgement."

The three men nodded and the King gestured to the page waiting at the door. As the page slowly turned the door handle, the trumpeter next to him blew three notes. The King winced. If there were anything he'd change about his position in life, it would be the trumpeter. Having to listen to that every time a door opened or closed was enough to weary anyone's nerves. He'd considered sacking the trumpeter but, as Queen Lorelei had pointed out, the man's family had been trumpeting for the King for three generations. He was probably already training his oldest son to take his place. Who was King Orel to put a whole family tree out of employment?

The first boy filed into the room and Master Blau announced Cedric of Longborough. He was the son of a Lordling over in the west country. Cedric bowed in his direction, sweeping the floppy brown hair from his eyes as he straightened.

"Right," said King Orel. "Ask whatever questions you need to ask."

And so it began. Slumping back on his cushioned throne, the King listened hard as Cedric answered each of the explorers in turn in his high, clear voice. Each boy would go through the same process until, at last, they would all return to the room for the final choosing.

King Orel sighed. It was going to be a long day.

~

Quinn watched as Anders hesitantly walked to the huge gilt door and disappeared through it, to the sound of trumpets. Blazes, but those trumpets got annoying after a while. Now he was the only one in the huge antechamber. The others had all gone through the door and disappeared.

Next it would be his turn.

The time between trumpets had differed. Cedric, the first candidate, had been in there for ages before the next boy was called. Ira, only a few minutes. Quinn presumed this was because the explorers needed only one look at the noble boy to tell that he was right for the task.

Quinn didn't hold out much hope that Anders would take up too much time – for all the opposite reasons to Ira.

Sure enough, the trumpets were sounding again and the gilt door was swinging inwards. He stood up, wiped his sweaty palms on his breeches and took a deep breath.

On the bright side, the whole ordeal was nearly over.

On the not-so-bright side, what happened next in this room would seal his fate for the next year. Home to his family and his books. Or not.

Master Blau was beckoning him impatiently and his feet were moving towards the door. And then he was there, bowing his head to the King and then turning to face the room, for his first sight of the three men who would decide his fate.

He recognized Dolan immediately. The man had visited every village in the land on his return from the Crusadic Wars, telling stories of daring-do and adventure – and Quinn's father still spoke of it. He'd been so impressed by the man that he'd parted with five precious centines to buy a signed drawing of Dolan, which had hung in the cottage hallway ever since. Jed had always loved hearing the Dolan stories his father told. Quinn, not so much.

The nobleman next to Dolan was not familiar to Quinn, but he looked rich enough to be powerful. He was certainly wearing those ridiculous puffy pants that all the aristocrats were parading in around the palace.

The only other man in the lineup was Zain, the Deslonder. Surely that was a mistake? Perhaps he was just holding a place for the real explorer.

"Any questions for this boy?" the King was asking.

Dolan looked him up and down, and shook his head emphatically. Quinn winced inwardly. It was one thing to decide you didn't want to be chosen – quite another to be dismissed so imperiously.

"Odilon?" the King asked.

The aristocrat stepped forward. "You are a farm boy, I believe?" he said, looking down his rather long nose at Quinn.

Quinn nodded. His voice had deserted him completely.

Odilon made a kind of harrumphing noise and retreated back to the line. Quinn had the feeling he hadn't made the aristocrat's list, which suited him just fine.

Now the Deslonder stepped forward. "What do you do around the farm?" he asked. His voice was deep and gravelly, but the tone was gentle.

Quinn was surprised. He had never heard the Deslonder speak – but the fact that he had confirmed he was the third explorer candidate. "I, er, help my mam," Quinn said, wincing as he did so. It was times like this that he wished he were able to say, as his brothers did, that he plowed fields by hand, maintained the barn, herded sheep. Manly pursuits. Truth be told, he *could* do all of those things (though the plowing wore him out well before he'd managed an entire field), but it wasn't considered to be his job. His job was to help his mam.

Dolan and Odilon hid smiles, but the Deslonder looked interested. "Doing what?" he asked.

Quinn sighed. Now he was for it. "Cooking, sewing, tending the chickens . . . that, er, sort of thing," he said.

He waited for the outbreak of laughter that usually followed this admission and, it had to be said, Dolan and Odilon were going very red in the face with their efforts to suppress their guffaws – but the laughter didn't come. Instead, the Deslonder simply nodded and stepped back into line.

“Nothing else?” the King asked. All three explorers shook their heads.

“Right then,” said the King, rubbing his hands together. “Let’s get all the boys back in and then you shall choose your scribes. Your boats leave on the evening tide.”

The trumpets did their thing again and the other nine students trooped back into the room. Cedric, Ira, Ajax, Norric, Blain, Sturand, Karol, Marcus and Anders. They fell into line beside Quinn and stood there. The tension in the room tightened several notches.

Quinn felt quite relaxed now that the others were here. Some of them were so impressive – Ira, Cedric, Norric and Blain, with their cool, haughty nobility, and Ajax with his sheer size and friendly grin; even Sturand, Karol and Marcus had their strengths (though Quinn didn’t think their maps were up to scratch at all). He and Anders didn’t stand a chance in this mix, he thought.

“Dolan, as the first competitor, you may choose your scribe first,” the King was saying.

The blond explorer stepped forward with military precision. He held himself true and straight, Quinn noted, as an ex-soldier would. If his boots were a little scuffed and his shirt fraying at the sleeves, well, that would surely just come down to the fact that he was a civilian now.

“I choose Ira,” he said.

Ira stepped forward to stand beside Dolan, showing no

surprise at being chosen – and chosen first. He would take that as his right, Quinn knew. Ira never lost.

"Right then, collect your things and report to the *Wandering Spirit* in one hour," the King told Ira. Quinn assumed the *Wandering Spirit* was Dolan's ship. "You leave tonight. Congratulations."

Ira bowed and, without acknowledging any of the other scribes, left the room.

"One down," said the King. "Odilon, you choose next."

The soft velvet of Odilon's tunic rustled as he minced forward in his uncomfortable-looking embroidered slippers. "I choose the redhead," he said.

Ajax! It was interesting that he hadn't called him by name, Quinn thought. But he knew that his red hair was one of Ajax's biggest draws. Ever since the red-haired General Isenheard had led the Verdanian army to victory over the Gelynions, securing a fragile peace between the two kingdoms more than fifty years before, red hair had been considered a good-luck charm.

Ajax stepped forward with a huge grin, no sign of any misgivings on his open, friendly face.

"Thank you," he said to Odilon, before bowing to the King.

The King laughed. "It's good to see some enthusiasm," he said.

Odilon smiled politely.

"Off you go then," said the King, waving them away languidly. "Report to the *Fair Maiden* in one hour."

As Ajax left the room, Quinn breathed out hard. Two down, one to go. Now the tension was almost unbearable. Cedric looked as though he would snap, he was so taut. As Ira's closest friend, he had been boasting for weeks about his chances for the race and Quinn knew that it would be a crushing blow were he not to be chosen.

Quinn fervently hoped that Cedric's dreams would not be crushed.

"Zain," the King said, softly. "Make your choice."

A long look passed between the two, before Zain stepped forward.

"I choose . . . Quinn, the farm boy," he said.

Quinn felt all the breath leave his body.

He stepped forward on shaky legs, fancying that he could feel Cedric's deadly looks piercing into his back. Part of him wanted to cry, even as another part of him, deep inside, was quietly pleased by the recognition. He'd never won anything before, and he guessed this qualified as a "win."

The Deslonder put out one huge hand and clamped it down on Quinn's shoulder. He bent down so that his eyes were level with Quinn's.

"I know you don't want to go," he said, keeping his voice low so that others could not hear. "If I could do without you, I would and send you back to your mam. But I can't."

Quinn nodded, gaze locked on that dark, scarred face.

"You have all that you need to succeed," the slave continued. "And you have something I need."

Quinn's mind raced. What did he have? It came to him in seconds. The Deslonder was the only one who knew about Quinn's memory. He'd been in the room at Markham on the day that Master Blau had selected him for the school. Since that day, his memory had not been spoken of again.

But Zain knew. And he thought it would give him an advantage in the race.

Quinn nodded slowly. He could not refuse to go. It would mean disobeying the King. And besides, his family would benefit from his participation in the race, whether he won or lost. But they'd be so much better off if Zain won.

If he had to be in this thing, no matter how terrified he was, then Quinn would hold true to the promise he'd made his father and he would do his best.

The Deslonder's eyes searched his face, seemed to like what he saw there, and then he straightened to face the King. Quinn followed his lead. The two heads bowed.

The King smiled. "Well, then, that's that," he said. "Report to the *Libertas* in one hour."

He turned to the other seven candidates, all standing forlornly at the back of the room. Six of them looked miserable; Anders, on the other hand, was struggling to contain his joy.

"You seven can also pack your bags," the King said. "You're going home. Master Blau, see that they are paid and dispatched as quickly as possible."

The old mapmaker nodded, rounding the seven boys up and ushering them from the room.

Quinn found himself in the unusual position of being almost alone with the King.

"Well, Zain, you've made your choice," the King said, his tone friendly. "Are you happy with it?"

The Deslonder nodded. "He'll do," he said.

A resounding vote of confidence, thought Quinn.

"And you, er, Quinn," the King said, turning to him. The jewels in his crown danced at they hit the light. "Are you looking forward to this adventure?"

Quinn paused. He didn't think it was etiquette to tell the King that he hated the whole idea and wanted to go home.

"Of c-c-course," he stammered.

"Hmm," said the King. "Your mother is Ellyn, daughter to Ralf, who was Baron of Cowl."

Quinn nodded. He didn't know much about his mam's family history, because she never spoke of it, but he knew that much.

"Interesting," said the King, surveying Quinn more closely. "He was a brave man, your grandfather. Foolish, perhaps, but strong in his convictions."

Quinn could only nod again, having no idea what the King was talking about.

"I hope that you have inherited that bravery," the King went on. "I suspect that you are going to need it – though you are in very good hands." He smiled fondly at the Deslonder.

Quinn stared. His questions about his family history were filed in the back of his mind to be examined later, while he contemplated the fact that the rumors about the King and Zain were true – these two *were* more like friends than master and slave.

Zain smiled, the sudden flash of white lightening his whole face. "We shall see," he said.

"We shall indeed," said the King. "For now the race begins!"

Trumpets sounded.

Quinn winced. He couldn't be sure, but for a second it looked as though King Orel did as well.

Chapter Four

He'd clearly done some enormous wrong in a previous existence. It was the only explanation for why he was here.

Quinn held on to the handrail for dear life, the solid wood under his hands a reminder that there were things in the world that did not roll, and pitch, and creak, and groan. Though not much, at this point, in his world.

He'd been aboard the *Libertas* for five days now and was still waiting for his sea legs to magically kick in. It seemed that all those hours sailing his skiff on the river with Aysha had done nothing to encourage this – not when faced with a deep, endless ocean.

The first mate, Cleaver, a crusty old salt with a bandanna and an ever-present pipe, assured him it would happen any moment now. Though he joked with the other crew members that Quinn's sea legs were the slowest to grow that he'd ever seen.

Quinn groaned as the ship began to climb up another wall of green, knowing that the trough on the other side would be deep – and that his stomach would be left somewhere near the top as the ship slid down the other side. Up above, the skies were blue and clear. Why then, was the sea so boiling mad?

If it weren't for all the tossing about, he'd be quite enjoying the voyage so far. He had his own snug little cabin, a desk, a good supply of writing implements and a pile of previous maps to research. The only trouble was, he hadn't been able to clear his head enough to do anything with any of it. The first two days at sea were a haze of nausea and headaches. He was on his feet now, but still next to useless.

Not that this was too much of a problem yet. They'd sailed west from Verdania and were still in territory that was familiar to most of the sailors on board. Their crew of six had been handpicked by Zain and was comprised mostly of slaves or former slaves. Quinn had been surprised by this, wondering how much experience they could have – but his doubts were soon assuaged when he realized that they'd all been around ships and sailing their whole lives. Even now, they worked in the King's dockyards. Their gratitude to Zain for choosing them for this expedition was touching and obvious.

Quinn was starting to get to know them all: Cleaver; Abel – tall, thin and a little clumsy, due in part, he suspected, to the size of his huge feet; Dilly – the smallest crew member, who could climb a mast faster than anyone; Ison – who didn't say a lot but was always first to act when an order was given; Jericho – with his huge smile and even larger moustache; and Cook – who worked miracles in the ship's small galley.

Also on board was Cleric Greenfield, sent along by the King to "supervise Zain." The bald little man had made it clear from day one that his role was merely nominal and that he would not interfere in the day-to-day running of the ship.

So far, so good.

There was just one dark cloud on this otherwise happy ship, and that was Zain himself. After those few words in the King's Counting House, the Deslonder had not troubled himself to speak to Quinn again. Looking at him now, standing behind the ship's helm, staring out over the rolling waves, Quinn wondered what he was thinking.

It was going to be a long and lonely voyage if the silence continued. The crew were friendly, but they kept to themselves, and Cleric Greenfield had spent most of his time so far in his cabin. Quinn thought he'd even be happy to see Ira at this point. At least it would give him someone his own age to talk to.

A sudden commotion down by the wheelhouse distracted him from these thoughts. Two crew members were struggling to drag a third towards the huge wooden wheel where Zain stood deep in thought. But who was it? The small, slight boy was putting up a big fight.

Curious, Quinn moved closer to the action.

"What's this?" asked Zain, eyes drifting from the horizon for only seconds.

"We found him below decks," growled Jericho, a short, squat man with an abundant dark moustache. Many of the crew were Deslonders and had names that Quinn had never heard before. "Hiding, he was. In the sacks of grain."

Zain inclined his head at Cleaver, who stepped up to take the helm, freeing him to focus on the problem at hand.

"The sacks of grain, eh?" he said, eyeing the prisoner balefully. "Comfortable, was it?"

"Yes!" came the defiant reply. "Very!"

Quinn stopped dead at the sound of that voice. He'd know it anywhere. She'd cut her hair, but this was no boy.

"Aysh–!" he called out involuntarily.

She rounded on him, talking over the top of him and cutting him off with a warning look. "Ay– what? Ay is for horses."

He got the message. "Er, where did you come from?" he asked, affecting nonchalance.

"A stowaway," said Jericho importantly, moustache bristling. "We found him below."

"We already established that," said Zain, looking back

and forth between Aysha and Quinn closely. "But you seem to know this boy, Quinn?"

Caught on the back foot, Quinn could only nod.

"Ah," said Zain, before turning back to Aysha. "The question then must be, what are you doing here? And how do you know *him*?"

It was Quinn's turn to shuffle as all eyes turned to him.

"Don't look at him," said Aysha. "He knows nothing about it. It was all me. I decided to come and I got myself here."

There was a note of pride in the last. Quinn's mouth twitched. Typical Aysha.

"Did you now?" Zain was saying. "The question is why and to what end."

"Get these buffoons to let me go and I'll tell you," said Aysha.

"Steady now," said Jericho. "A little less of the buffoon, thanks very much."

"Right," said Abel. "That's a bit harsh." He looked genuinely offended.

"Er, yes, quite," said Aysha, realizing that being rude to her captors might not be the best course of action right now. "Sorry. Anyway, can we just sit down and I'll tell you?"

Zain nodded. "Let, er, him, go," he said. "Let's get this sorted as quickly as possible. But it had better be a good story – you do know what happens to stowaways on the King's ships, don't you?"

It was at this point that Quinn realized just how menacing the Deslonder could be. Aysha began to look very worried.

"Er, no, not exactly," she said.

Zain stared pointedly at the sea. "They go overboard," he said. "Of course."

Quinn nodded without thinking. It made sense – no ship needed an extra mouth to feed. Aysha glared at him, and he quickly stilled his head.

"Right, that will be all for now, Jericho and Abel. I'll call you if I need you." The crew members wandered off, muttering to each other.

"You two, in here." He led them inside the wheelhouse, a small space located directly behind the helm, in which the captain of a ship could sit, protected from the wind, and do whatever it was that captains did.

Glancing around, Quinn noticed that Zain had copies of the six existing world maps nailed to the walls. He winced to see the precious vellum treated so casually but acknowledged that it was probably the safest place for them.

So engrossed was he in examining the maps before him – larger copies than the ones that he himself had been given – that he nearly missed the conversation unfolding between Aysha and Zain.

"Well, now, missy, best you explain yourself." Zain's scarred face was impassive, but his voice brooked no argument.

Quinn and Aysha both gaped at him. "How did you know?" sputtered Aysha.

Zain snorted. "I have a little more experience in such matters than Jericho and Abel," he said. "But that's beside the point. The question is, why are you *really* here? This isn't some kind of misguided love thing, is it?"

"Leif's boots, no!" Quinn and Aysha both spoke at once.

Zain almost smiled. Almost. "Very well, then. Why? What possible good can it do you to stow away on a boat that's going to sea for a year and then returning right back to where you started?"

We hope, Quinn added silently.

Aysha took a moment to compose her thoughts. "For starters, I just don't think it's fair that boys get to do all the fun stuff," she said. "They didn't even consider trying girls out for the mapmakers' school."

Zain looked bemused. "But it's always been that way," he said.

"Yes, well, that doesn't mean that things can't change," she said. "Look at you. You've been a slave for most of your life. But you're not just going to accept that, are you? You're here."

Quinn wasn't sure whether bringing up the slave thing was such a great idea, but Zain nodded once.

"You have a point," he said. "And your second point?"

"Second?" Aysha looked confused.

"Well, you said 'for starters,'" said Zain. "I'm assuming that wasn't your sole argument."

"Er, no, of course not," said Aysha, looking around in such a way that Quinn knew she was making it up as she went along. Then she stilled, and seemed to decide something. "The truth is," she said to Zain, and suddenly her eyes were pleading, "I've got no one. My mother died, well, of a broken heart, I think, and I've been alone ever since. I didn't even realize how lonely I was until Quinn came to the kitchen garden and found me working there. I knew he'd be chosen for this journey, even if he didn't."

She stopped and she and Zain both looked Quinn up and down in way that made him feel like the ants he and Aysha sometimes studied in the woods.

"I didn't want to be left alone again," she continued. "So on the day of the decision I packed my bag and headed down to the docks to wait. I knew that the word would spread quickly down there about who had been chosen, and by whom, and I was right. I knew it was Quinn before you, Mr. Zain, even showed up and I was well in position before you set sail."

Quinn was impressed.

Zain looked less so. "It's a sad story and you show great

ingenuity," he said. "But that doesn't change the fact that you've stowed away. A crime punishable by death."

"Only if I'm not a crew member," said Aysha, pleading. "Surely you could find a use for me."

"I cannot have a girl on this ship," said Zain, shaking his head. "The others would never allow it. Everyone knows girls are bad luck on a boat."

"Not exactly," said Quinn, thinking furiously, trying to come up with something that would save Aysha. "That only became the case about, er, fifty years ago. And it had more to do with bad luck. It just so happened that a ship with the head cleric on board just so happened to hit some rocks when a girl just so happened to be steering it. Really, it could have happened to anyone. But the cleric saw it as a sign and that was that. Up till then, girls and women were on board ships all the time."

"You know this how?" asked Zain.

"I read it in a book once," said Quinn.

Zain gave him a long, hard look.

Quinn tried to look innocent. He knew that Zain wouldn't question his memory. Just days before, Cleaver had jokingly shown Quinn twenty different seaman's knots at lightning speed – all part of "helping those sea legs to grow." Quinn had laughed along and pretended to fumble just one of them, but, as soon as the older sailor had gone back to his post, Quinn had sat down in a quiet corner with the rope and gone through each and every knot perfectly – only to look up minutes later to find Zain's eyes on him.

No, Zain wouldn't question his memory, but whether that would be enough to throw off years of sailors' superstition was another question.

"I might ask to see that book once we return," Zain said, tapping his fingers on the desk.

"Of course," said Quinn. He knew from past experience that most people didn't remember their threats from one week to the next – by the time they returned to Verdania in a year, Zain would have no recollection of this conversation. He hoped – given that no such book existed.

"Even so," the Deslonder continued, "I don't see how I'd convince the crew that something that Quinn *says* he once read in a book should undermine something they've always known."

Even Aysha was quiet at that. Which worried Quinn more than anything.

"They don't need to know," said Quinn firmly. "Even Jericho and Abel didn't guess it. In her breeches, and with her hair cut like that . . ."

Zain was nodding. "True," he said. "But the crew will expect her to sleep below with them, and it will be harder to hide down there."

The crew slept below decks in a series of hammocks, which swung gently in rhythm with the ship's movements. Quinn had often thought that they looked more comfortable than his own little wooden bed, built in to his cabin and with a side rail that kept him from falling out when the weather got wilder.

"Couldn't I sleep in here?" asked Aysha, looking around. "You could tell them that I get . . . seasick and need the fresh air."

Zain looked thoughtful. "Hmm. Do you know plant craft?"

Aysha hesitated. Admitting such knowledge had been her mother's undoing. Quinn watched as she considered her next move. Zain sat unmoving and Aysha seemed to be picking him apart with her eyes. She'd always been a good judge of people, Quinn knew.

She came to a decision. "Yes," she said, slowly. "I am a healer."

Zain smiled. "Then that shall be your job. You can sleep in here and help Quinn with his information and knowledge gathering."

Aysha closed her eyes with relief. "Thank you, Mr. Zain. Oh, thank you."

"But," Zain continued, "there are two provisos."

Quinn and Aysha stood to attention.

"One is that none of the crew finds out you're a girl."

They nodded.

"And the second is that you drop the mister business," the Deslonder said. "I am no mister. I am Zain."

Aysha nodded. "Seems the least I can do under the circumstances," she said, straight-faced.

There was a pause. Quinn held his breath. Given that Zain hadn't proved the chattiest of men over the preceding week, he wasn't sure how he'd take Aysha's quip.

Zain's laugh boomed out suddenly, like a foghorn, just once. "I like you, girl," he said, before sobering just as suddenly, "but bear in mind that I will do nothing to jeopardize this mission. You cause trouble and I will leave you on the nearest shore."

Aysha swallowed hard.

"However," Zain continued, in what Quinn realized was his longest speech to date, "I suspect it will be good for my homesick scribe to have you around. Keep your head down and all will be well."

He paused. "We're going to need to change your name. Any suggestions?"

"I think we should keep it simple," said Aysha. "Quinn shouted out 'Ash,' or near enough, when he saw me. I'll be Ash."

Zain nodded again. "Ash, it is. And now I must get back to the business of actually running this ship. We will continue our course west, Quinn, for the time being. I know we have reached the extreme of known maps, but I see no reason to change our current tack."

Quinn said nothing. He'd been watching their progress daily via his copies of the existing maps, checking them against the information that the crew was feeding him. Measurements, star readings, visual sightings of the coastline – they'd been trying to ensure Quinn had as much information as possible. All of this was helping him to build a more thorough picture of where they were.

Only now there was no more map. They were heading out onto the wide blue water, into unknown territory. There was just ocean, stars and his compass – and whatever intuition and knowledge he'd managed to pick up in three months of studying with Master Blau.

Which, Quinn decided, was probably not enough.

Chapter Five

"Sail ho!"

The shout echoed around the *Libertas*, and Quinn, tucked up in his cabin working on calculations and recording his thoughts, stood up, startled.

They'd seen nothing but water for two weeks now. Each day had dissolved into the next, the only difference being the color of the water (very deep blue now) and occasional squall. He hadn't even seen a bird for three days, and Quinn reckoned this was simply because they were too far from land for any bird to be able to fly the distance. It was a sobering thought.

And now a sail. He jumped up, slid his boots on over the warm, woolen socks his mother had made him, and thumped out of his cabin and up the stairs to the deck. Ash had beaten him to it.

"What do you see?" she shouted up to Dilly, high atop the mainsail on a tiny wooden platform. Dilly was quick and agile, and was often sent scampering up the mast to scan the horizon. He, and even the bigger, older crew members, made it look easy, the climb up and down that mast, and Quinn had been practicing on the smaller masts so that he, too, could take his turn at watch. But he was yet to take on the largest mast.

Still, he had a good head for heights and, while he wasn't as obviously muscular as his brothers, he'd discovered that his wiry strength, honed from many years of work around the farm, carrying heavy loads for his mother and, of course, sailing the skiff and climbing trees with Aysha, was right at home on a ship.

Particularly now that he'd finally "grown" his sea legs.

"Sail!" Dilly shouted back. "Looks like one of ours."

King Orel had insisted that each of the explorer's ships flew one flag in the Verdanian national colors of red and blue. This allowed them to keep track of each other without necessarily getting too close (not that this would be difficult, Quinn reasoned, when there were so few boats out here).

Zain joined Ash and Quinn in the bow, spyglass in hand.

"Looks like the *Wandering Spirit* to me," he said. "And I don't think she's pleased to see us."

He handed the looking glass to Quinn, who put it to his eye. He could see the hive of activity on board the *Wandering Spirit* as crew scurried back and forth.

"What are they doing?" he asked, handing the glass to Ash.

"Preparing to haul in, by the looks of things," said Zain, thoughtfully. "Looks as though there's a big change of direction coming."

Sure enough, as they watched, the *Wandering Spirit* began a swooping turn, which took her from heading due west, as the *Libertas* was, to a new setting due north.

"Where could they be going?" asked Ash.

Quinn flicked through his mind, thinking hard, before shaking his head. "No idea," he said. "I can't think of any reason to go that way."

Zain smiled. "There's no reason to go this way, either," he said. "Nothing but hope and luck. They've obviously decided to leave it to us and try their luck in another direction."

They stood and watched the *Wandering Spirit* as she sailed away, leaving nothing but churning water in her wake.

Hours later, the ship was still in view, the horizon extended before her. Quinn was glad that they could still see her. Despite the haste with which the other company had fled, he felt comforted by the knowledge that they were not alone out on the vast inkiness of the ocean.

The sun set and the moon rose. He went below to mark another day off on his cabin wall. And to write up his thoughts on the day in the calfskin notebook that Master Blau had given him as a farewell gift.

"Use it well," he'd said on the dock, and Quinn had nodded, humbled at receiving such an expensive gift.

At first, Quinn had thought it was empty, a place to record his impressions and thoughts of the journey. Then he'd realized there was a letter tucked into the back cover. His first letter ever!

Quinn

Congratulations on your selection. If I know you, right now you're not thinking of yourself as blessed, but cursed. Still your thoughts. All things happen for a reason.

Zain has chosen you because he sees in you what I see in you: a clever, resourceful boy who will be a valuable asset to his team. Stay true to who you are and all will be well.

Master Blau

All will be well. Quinn read those words to himself every night before he went to bed.

He read back over the previous entries in his journal, all recorded on one page.

No land today.

No land today.

No land today.

And so on. At least tonight he had something to report.

Ship today.

He paused, wondering again about that sudden change in direction. It was as though the *Wandering Spirit* had seen something that spooked them. Surely the sight of the *Libertas* wasn't enough for that. If they took fright every time they saw a competitor's ship, they were going to end up on a very convoluted course around the world.

He was distracted by a shout from the watch. This time, it wasn't as clear.

Another ship?

He cocked his head, listening. But there was only silence.

Wondering, he slid his boots back on again and stole silently into the passageway. He was supposed to be in bed now. Zain liked all crew members tucked up soon after nightfall. The only ones awake and about were the captain or first mate, who maintained the ship's direction and progress, and the lookout on the mast.

The garbled shout came again. This time he didn't hesitate, sneaking up the stairs and out onto the deck under the stars. Zain was standing at the bottom of the tall mast, Ash beside him. Sleeping where she did, she would not have missed the shout.

"Get down here," Zain was saying in a harsh whisper. There was a scuffling noise above, and then Quinn heard the usual slide-thump noise that accompanied a man's progress up or down the mast.

Jericho slid down the last few feet of the mast and landed with a whoosh at Zain's feet. He slumped there, as though all strength had left him.

"*What did you see?*" asked Zain, in the tone of a man who was repeating himself for the umpteenth time.

Jericho looked up at his captain, eyes rolling in fear. "A monster!" he said. "Huge! Breathing fire!"

Zain looked out over the calm sea. The moon was fat and round, casting enough light to see clearly.

"I see nothing," he said to the man at his feet.

"It comes and goes," said Jericho. "Up and down, closer and closer."

There was another pause. "I still see nothing," said Zain. "You need to get back up there for another look."

"No!" shouted Jericho, clutching the mast. "I will not look upon the devil from the deep again." It was clear he wasn't going anywhere.

Zain looked around again, spotting Quinn lurking in the shadow of the wheelhouse.

"You! Quinn! Can you climb this mast?"

Quinn gulped. He could climb the smaller mast, in broad daylight, with all the time in the world. Going up the large one – which was at least twice as high – at night, with Zain watching every move from below, was quite a different story.

"Er . . ." he hesitated.

Ash rolled her eyes at him as she dug hard in his ribs with her pointy elbow. "Yes, he can," she said to Zain. "And if he can't, I will."

She knew he wouldn't refuse a direct challenge.

"Get up there," Zain said to him. "Tell me what you see."

Quinn had no choice. He began to climb, hand over hand, feet following, concentrating on keeping an easy, regular rhythm. All went well for the first minute or so . . . before his right foot slipped on the polished pole and he slid all the way back to the ground.

"An impressive start," said Zain, his scarred face showing no expression as he looked down at the boy at his feet. "Try again."

As much as he wanted to simply give up at that point and go back to the comfort of his bed, Quinn was curious. What had Jericho seen? Could there really be a monster this far out to sea? Plus, he knew that if he didn't make it this time, Ash would step over him as she climbed the mast herself.

He began again.

He could hear his own breath as he climbed. The closer he got to the top, the more the wind seemed to blow, giving the whole mast a gentle sway. He looked up – not far now. From below, the wooden platform on which the lookout sat seemed very small. But once you got up here, it looked enormous. A safe haven. He refused to look down. Looking down would simply show him how far he had to fall. Onto the hard, wooden planks of the deck. Every bone in his body breaking into tiny pieces.

No, looking up was by far the best option.

Reaching the wooden platform, Quinn climbed through the hole to one side, then slid himself across to the other, wider side. He glanced around – and could feel himself gape.

Up here, he truly got an idea of just how wide this ocean was. From horizon to horizon and beyond. Nothing but inky blackness dotted with the whitecaps that reflected in the moonlight. A trail of light led his eyes from the water to the moon, like a silvery staircase dancing on the surface.

Above him, the velvety darkness was strewn with stars. They seemed much brighter up here. He glanced down at the ship's deck far below him. The wooden ship, which had seemed so big when he'd first seen it, reminded him of the wine bottle cork his mam had given him to play with as a child. He'd put it in a bowl of water and watch it bob up and down, amazed by how it floated.

The ship seemed even smaller.

Staring about him, he remembered that moment in the kitchen garden when he'd stood under the sky – the same sky they floated under now? – and wondered how it could spread all the way around the world and be below him.

Now he was beginning to grasp just how very big this world might turn out to be.

"Can you see anything?" Ash's voice floated up to him on the breeze.

“No,” he answered automatically, still recovering from the shock of his own insignificance. “No . . . wait . . .” He returned his attention to the task at hand and began scanning the horizon, searching for Jericho’s “monster.”

It didn’t take long to come up with an answer. “Nothing!” he shouted back.

“Give it a few more minutes,” came Zain’s voice. “Jericho said it went up and down. Maybe it’s down.”

Quinn sighed. Despite the grandeur of the view up here, he wasn’t very comfortable. When he’d first arrived on board he’d been given one piece of advice by Cleaver, the first mate: one hand for you, one hand for the ship. Basically, hold on to something at all times.

While his sea legs had developed to the point where he could walk around on deck with both hands free unless the waves were really rolling, up here he was clinging to that advice. Literally.

He wiggled around on the platform until his back was against the mast, still clutching it tightly in his left hand. This might be what flying felt like, he thought, as the wind caught his hair and the ship rocked beneath him. If he held his arms out like the wings on a bird, he might even take off . . .

Suddenly, his eye was caught by a movement off the starboard bow. A flash of white.

Quinn squinted in the darkness, eyes glued to the spot.

There it was again. It looked a bit like the whoosh of the fountain near the pleached walk in the King's garden. He remembered watching the angel at the center of the fountain spitting water up in the air and wondering what it was all about.

Had Jericho seen an angel?

"There's something out there," he shouted down to Zain and Ash on the deck below. "A fountain."

There was a pause, before Ash's laughter floated up to him. "A fountain? Out here in the middle of nowhere?"

Personally, he preferred his version to the fire-breathing monster that Jericho had seen, but he could see her point. "Well, take a look yourself," he said. "Off to starboard."

He watched as they rushed to the starboard rail and then returned his eyes to the water. Just in time to see a huge white shape rear up out of the water, close enough to splash water over the deck and set the ship to violent rocking. Quinn threw both arms around the mast and held on for dear life, watching as the monster – for what else could it be? – fell back into the waves with a resounding *slap*.

"Quinn! Quinn! Are you all right?" Zain was calling from down below, where he was attempting to help Ash stand upright, while keeping them both secured to the ship's rail. The rest of the crew, plus Cleric Greenfield, had rushed up on deck, amidst much shouting and jostling.

"I'm okay. Still here!" Shaking like a leaf, but still here.

"What was it?" Zain shouted. "I've never seen anything so big!"

Quinn grimaced. He'd been half hoping that Zain, with his many years' life experience, would be able to say, "Oh that, it's just a barnacle-jumper," or something. But apparently not. "I couldn't really tell," Quinn shouted back. "It all happened so fast. Er, can I come down now?"

"Can you still see it?"

Quinn cast a cautious eye about, scanning the sea around them while retaining his close relationship with the mast. "No, I can't see it," he said. "It must have been –"

Whatever he was about to say was lost in another huge rush of water as the monster surfaced again, this time even closer to the ship. Quinn watched in amazement and horror as the huge beast reared up out of the water, reaching a height nearly halfway up the tall mast where he was perched. The long, pointed, white horn on its head slashed the night sky.

Just how big was this thing? And what would it do next?

He was answered seconds later when it again fell back into the waves with that echoing, slapping sound.

The silence that followed was broken only by the creaking and groaning of the *Libertas* as she again pitched and rolled, riding the wake left by the monster, and the quavering voice of Cleric Greenfield, as he prayed for their souls.

With his eyes on the spot where the beast had disappeared, Quinn began counting.

By the time he hit fifty, there was movement again. This time, it was a fountain of water, whooshing straight up into the air, reaching almost as high as the animal itself had risen. This must be what Jericho had meant when he said the monster was "fire-breathing" – where Quinn saw water, he'd seen smoke.

Quinn saw a great head rise up out of the ocean, white all over, with a small black dot for an eye. The swordlike horn he'd spotted lay along the surface of the water as the beast appeared to look them over. Quinn thanked heaven for the bright moon that night – otherwise all this whooshing and slapping and splashing would be going on out in the dark night with them all left to wonder what was happening.

One thing was certain: the creature didn't seem interested in attacking them. Had it wanted to, it could simply have performed one of its backflips onto the deck of the *Libertas* and taken them all down with it. Instead, it was languidly floating off the starboard bow. Weighing them up, thought Quinn.

Then it was gone. From his lofty height, Quinn saw the great head dive down and then, seconds later, an enormous, fish-shaped tail fin appeared. It slapped the water three times, like a round of applause, and then was gone, leaving only a frothing trail of bubbles in its wake.

Quinn stayed at his station, wondering, for another thirty minutes, listening to the babble of voices below as the crew tried to work out what had happened. Then he unfolded his numb muscles and climbed gingerly back down the mast. There would be no further sign of the "monster" tonight, he thought. It had made its point. Had this been what the *Wandering Spirit* had seen? The thing that had spooked the crew and sent them haring off to the north?

Quinn could only suppose it was. He wasn't sure whether to feel spooked or not. At first glance, the creature had been terrifying, but apart from splashing around a bit, it had made no move to hurt them. If anything, it seemed only to want to let them know it was there, to show that they weren't alone out there on the waves. A benevolent spirit from the deep, sent to watch over them, perhaps?

He could see Zain and Ash at the bottom of the mast, anxious, perplexed faces upturned as he made his descent. The rest of the crew huddled around, whispering. A watch had been posted at the bow and the stern, swinging oil lanterns to signify their presence.

It was going to be a long night.

Chapter Six

The sun beat down, a hazy yellow dot in a seamless blanket of bright blue, taking the edge off the cool air. Quinn scratched himself lazily, shifting his position on the wooden deck to relieve the pressure on his hip. Stretching out one arm to block the sun, he realized his skin had been burned a deep caramel brown.

Six weeks at sea would do that to a person.

He wiggled his bare feet, enjoying the warmth on his toes. Zain would not be impressed, being a man who kept his boots on at all times, possibly even in bed, though Quinn could not confirm this. "A man cannot move quickly in bare feet," Zain would say if he saw Quinn now. "And you never know when you'll need to move quickly."

He had a point, Quinn thought. But given the slow pace of their progress, he couldn't really see that there'd be need for speedy movement any time soon.

He yawned. He'd been taking his turn as lookout ever since the Night of the Monster. Regardless of their vigilance that night, and every day and night since, they'd seen no further sign of the great beast. Quinn wasn't sure whether to be happy or sad about that. He'd quite like another look at the creature from the deep. But he was a minority of one. Everyone else on board would be happy to never see it again.

Fortunately, though, it seemed as though the beast – he really ought to give it a better name than that – had been a good omen, rather than bad, despite the fact that it had scared them all witless. Since its appearance, they'd had one perfect sailing day after another. The ocean was as smooth as the little lake in the King's garden, the sun shone brightly, a stiff light breeze prevailed. For weeks.

And yet they still hadn't found land.

On the plus side, they hadn't yet sailed off the edge of the world either, so Quinn was happy enough.

He scratched again – lice were, unfortunately, non-paying passengers on every ship, no matter how clean. He had to admit that Zain ran a tight ship. Talking to the other crew members, he'd learned that the Deslonder had been a fighting captain of some repute before the Crusadic Wars. Though young, he'd run his own ship and earned the deep scars on his face during some mighty battles in the East.

His capture by King Orel had come about only because he'd returned home to protect his own village.

How must it feel for such a proud man, a warrior, to have been taken into slavery?

Quinn had taken to studying the Deslonder when he thought he wasn't watching. Zain still held himself like a soldier, tall and upright. His presence was commanding – his sheer size was no small point in that – but he rarely shouted. In the same way that he had calmed Quinn at the choosing by telling him he was needed, Zain managed to make every man on his crew feel their role was vital. And so they didn't hesitate to play it.

Look at Quinn now, high in the air above the ship, looking for land that didn't exist.

It was the same respect that made them all roll out of their bunks at the crack of dawn to do the "training" that Zain had insisted, on day one at sea, they all undertake. He was teaching them the fighting moves that had made the Deslonders' reputation as some of the fiercest warriors in the world. A system of kicks, punches and throws that meant even someone as slight as Quinn could be a force to be reckoned with – without a weapon. Or so Zain told him. Quinn had his doubts.

Nonetheless, he turned up to training every morning, going through the set routine of warm-up exercises, practicing his punching against the large, man-sized bag that Zain had created using one of the crew's duffel bags. It was filled with a mix of the sandbags they used for ballast in the hold and some extra bedding. They practiced sweeping kicks, grappling moves, and ducking and weaving. Every once in a while, Zain would rush at one of them with a large stick held high and attempt to hit them with it, while the hapless victim tried to defend himself. Quinn particularly disliked these sessions, having felt the hard sting of that stick on his shoulder or arm one too many times.

"In a real fight, I would have just cut off your arm," Zain would say. "Again."

And so they'd do it again.

Quinn was proud of the fact that he carried fewer bruises from those sessions now. He was also much better at staying on his feet, after Zain's continuous drills in balance exercises, hopping around the ship on first one leg and then the other (not easy when the swell was up), or simply trying to stand and walk on a thin wooden beam that Zain had fixed between the masts. Quinn had proved surprisingly good at that exercise – as had Ash. He supposed wandering around the rafters of the Freeman family barn, spying on his brother Simon and Merryn, the blacksmith's daughter, went some way to explaining that.

Quinn still wasn't sure what good all this training was going to do him, but he definitely felt stronger and fitter than when he'd left Verdania. No mean feat given the size of the ship.

He could thank the size of the ship, however, for his increasing proficiency in understanding the language of Deslond. Close proximity with the crew meant he was picking up words and phrases, filing them away in his memory and drawing the necessary threads together for understanding, without the Deslonders even realizing. Quinn saw no reason, at this stage, to let on that he knew when they were laughing at him. At least he knew that, so far, no one had guessed Ash's secret – or his.

Quinn sighed, and rolled over onto his back. He was so comfortable up here now that he rarely bothered to hold on, and he timed his progress up the mast each day, counting under his breath.

He wished he could close his eyes. There was nothing to see after all. But falling asleep on a narrow platform on a rolling boat wasn't the best plan. Falling off would be fatal. Best he sit up.

He was wiggling up to sitting position when he saw the bird. Soaring in lazy circles overhead, great wings spread wide. He'd never seen a bird like it before, its white feathers glistening in the sun. He wondered what kind of bird –

Leif's boots! A *bird*! That meant . . .

His eyes scanned the horizon wildly, looking, searching – there! The faintest outline of a dark spot.

He jumped to his feet. "Land!" he screamed. "Land ho! It's land! Northwest!"

Down below he could hear running and shouting as everyone on board made their way to the bow.

As for Quinn, he didn't take his eyes off that dark dot.

They weren't sailing off the edge of the world. Not today.

~

Night was beginning to fall and the crew was getting edgy. To be this close to solid ground, and not be able to find a suitable landing place, was making everyone snappy.

Quinn and Ash, hanging over the port bow, stayed well out of the way, keeping a weather eye out for rocks. And there were plenty. The soaring cliffs that stretched overhead were shored up at the bottom with a carpet of boulders and jagged outcrops, which appeared suddenly under the sucking waves. Zain had kept the ship well off the shoreline and Quinn was using his prime position to make mental notes as they made their way north. Zain had chosen their direction with the simple flip of a centine. As he put it, there was no gain to be made either way at this stage, as they had no idea where they were.

Wherever they'd ended up, it was a wild and majestic land, Quinn thought, watching the waves crash white and frothy on the dark cliffs. Granite, he thought, remembering a book that Cleric Redland had given him once on rocks and crystals. Stands of trees could be seen, as tall and sturdy as the oak trees that grew near his home in Markham. What lay beyond these cliffs, those trees? He could only imagine at this stage, as none of the small coves they'd seen so far were suitable for a ship the size of the *Libertas*.

He sighed. As fond as he was of the *Libertas*, the sight of land had given him itchy feet. He wanted more than anything to be off the ship and to feel the sand between his toes. He wanted to eat something different from the salt pork and gruel that had sustained them after their fresh vegetable supplies ran out. Most of all, he wanted to sleep on a bed that didn't rock and roll under him.

He shoved the hair out of his eyes. Despite Ash's best efforts with the small, sharp knife she'd "borrowed" (as she put it) from the King's kitchen, his hair was too long. He didn't mind – he preferred it that way, truth be told, and was happy to tie it back with a piece of leather thong – but he knew his mam would be horrified if she saw him now.

"There!" Ash shouted suddenly, gesturing wildly to the left. "There!"

And he saw it too. The cliffs suddenly ended and there was a cove, fringed by white sand. The water remained dark blue until well inside the cove, hinting that it was deep enough for the *Libertas*, before gradually lightening to the shore. Quinn knew that Zain would check the depth of the water in the cove using a lead line, to be absolutely sure there were no lurking dangers for the ship.

He made another mental note to check the navigation charts and calculations that he and Zain were updating between them for an exact reading on the location of this cove. Tomorrow he would add it to the information he was compiling for his map. He'd already used information such as the average daily ship's speed, star positions, direction and what Zain called "dead reckoning" – the small amount of information on the course they had combined with Zain's gut feel for the drift of the ocean – to estimate the distance they'd just traveled. Now Quinn needed to begin to position this land, whatever it was. He was looking forward to climbing to the top of those huge cliffs to try to get an idea of the scope and scale of this coastline. Was this just a small island they'd discovered, or was it something larger?

As they sailed into the cove, though, they discovered that it was larger and deeper than it looked.

"The *Fair Maiden* is already here!" Quinn cried, disappointed that they weren't the first.

But how long had Odilon and Ajax been here? There'd been no sign of them on the ocean.

Quinn thought fast. Technically, the *Fair Maiden* was a much faster ship than the *Libertas*. She was bigger, with an extra mast that gave her extra power. The probability was that the other crew had been anchored here for several days. But why?

Zain obviously had doubts of his own. "I think we should approach with caution," he said, as he steered the *Libertas* through the shoals at the entrance to the cove. "That camp on the beach looks well established – and deserted."

Quinn now saw that there was a makeshift tent village tucked behind the *Fair Maiden*. All was still. Nothing moved on board the ship either. It was as though the crew had vanished. Even if they'd gone to explore the surrounding area, they'd have left a lookout.

"We'll anchor nearby, but not too close, and then we'll row over to see what's going on," said Zain, casually.

We? Quinn sincerely hoped that "we" didn't include him.

"Put your boots on," said Zain, looking over at him. "And tell Jericho and Abel to prepare the longboat."

Apparently "we" meant him as well.

"Wouldn't you rather I stayed here and began work on my map?" he asked, trying to keep the desperation out of his voice.

Zain smiled, though there was no humor in it. "No," he said. "You've been on board the *Fair Maiden*. I need you to tell me if there's anything amiss."

It was true. On the day they'd left, while the King made speeches and the band played, the three scribes had been invited to tour each other's ships. Ira had declined, intimating that such childish behavior was beneath him, though Quinn suspected that this was more to do with avoiding Quinn than any great maturity. Ajax and Quinn, both nervous, had taken up the opportunity willingly. If nothing else, it had given them a chance to have a few words.

The *Fair Maiden* was, as Quinn expected, a well-appointed, well-maintained vessel. No expense had been spared in either her fit-out or her finishes. Next to her, the *Libertas* had looked plain, but Quinn knew that Zain had chosen her from a selection of ships the King had offered him. The Deslonder must have had his reasons.

Ajax had shown Quinn all over the *Fair Maiden*, so he had an exact picture of the ship's layout in his mind.

"What do you think of this?" Ajax had asked, throwing open the door to his cabin. It was twice the size of Quinn's own.

"I've never had so much space to myself in my life!" Ajax had gone on, looking as though he were wondering what to do with it all.

"Well, you are a growing boy," Quinn had joked, trying to lighten the mood. They'd both laughed and then run, harum-scarum, over the rest of the ship, gaping at some of the more extravagant touches, such as the gold door handles.

Now Quinn found himself hoping that his friend was okay.

~

The splash of oars hitting the water was the only sound in the longboat. Packed in with Zain, the two crewmen, a barrel of fresh water – one of their last, and the huge sword that Zain had pulled out from under the tiller, Quinn wondered what he was getting himself into.

He was carrying Ash's kitchen knife, tucked down into his boot. Like every Verdanian boy his age, he had basic skills with a knife, taught to him by his father. "Nobody will defend our farm unless we do," his da had told them all, and drilled them until he was satisfied they could at least grip and throw a knife without harming themselves in the process. Unfortunately, knives were expensive, so each boy had been presented with one on his sixteenth birthday. Still two years off for Quinn.

Really, though, how irresponsible was it for his parents to send him off around the world without a knife? He conveniently overlooked the fact that everyone, including him, had assumed he would not be chosen for the race.

Jed and Simon had added some sword skills to their repertoire, but they were self-taught, using wooden swords they'd fashioned from broken ax handles. It was only nobility who got to learn to use a sword properly.

And, apparently, Deslonders.

He fingered the knife handle, watching as the *Fair*

Maiden loomed larger and larger. All remained quiet on deck.

"I don't like this, Captain," said Jericho, as he reached forward to pull the oars back. "They should have seen us by now."

Zain nodded, eyes fixed on the deck of the *Fair Maiden*.

"Maybe they're just all ashore," said Abel between puffs as he labored to keep up with Jericho. "Exploring, like."

"Without a lookout?" Disdain made Jericho stop briefly, destroying the rhythm of the oars and checking their speed. One look from Zain, and the pair were pulling together again.

"Tell me what you see, Quinn," Zain said, low and slow.

Quinn ran his glance over the ship, from bow to stern. "Four sails tied neatly. No damage to the bow. No one in the wheelhouse. No lookouts posted."

"Does she look the same as when you last saw her?"

Quinn summoned up the image of that last day at the docks. "Yes," he said. "No, wait!" He thought furiously. "There was a large pile of extra lines stored on hooks on the side of the wheelhouse," he said. "Big loops of rope. They're not there."

Zain nodded. They rowed on in silence, pulling around the bow and presenting to the port side of the *Fair Maiden*. A rope ladder dangled over the side, suggesting that someone had gone ashore.

"We'll go up and check it out," Zain told Jericho and Abel. "Keep the boat steady here until we return."

Without waiting for an answer, he began to scramble up the rope, Quinn following behind.

On board, the silence grew only more eerie. "Hallo!" Zain called. His voice echoed around the empty deck.

"They're not here," said Quinn, shifting from foot to foot, trying to quell his nerves. "They must have all gone ashore."

"Odilon is many things," said Zain. "But a fool he is not. He would not leave his ship – his home and the only method of transport he has – unguarded while he went ashore." He drew his sword. "Come, we will check below deck."

As they went down into the belly of the ship, Quinn kept his eyes open. And it wasn't long before he noticed another difference between this and his last visit. "Zain," he whispered. "The door handles."

Zain glanced at the door closest. "There are no door handles," he said.

"Yes, but there were. Solid gold ones."

Silence.

"On a ship?" Zain asked, quizzical.

Quinn nodded, then realized Zain couldn't see him. In the narrow passage, he was tucked in behind the Deslonder.

"I thought it strange, but Ajax told me that Odilon has gold door handles in all his homes. He was bringing the comfort with him. Now there's no comfort."

"Hmm," said Zain. He hurried ahead, pushing open doors as he went. There were only a few – the crew slept down in the hull, as they did on the *Libertas*. "Okay. We've seen enough."

Relieved, Quinn turned back to the daylight and within minutes they were back in the longboat and rowing hard for the *Libertas*. "We'll collect the others and head for shore," said Zain. "I'll leave Cleric Greenfield and Ash on board to secure the boat."

He clearly wasn't expecting trouble.

Within the hour, it was done and the now fully laden longboat was nearing the beach. Ash had been less than impressed with remaining on board, but had quickly realized the futility of arguing with Zain, and had settled down with Cleric Greenfield in the bow to watch from a safe distance. She liked the cleric, Quinn knew, and she wouldn't have wanted him left on his own.

Quinn wished he were taking a front-row seat as well, rather than diving headlong into the action.

They pulled the boat up into the fine, dusty sand, a little upwind from the makeshift camp on the beach. Silently, weapons drawn, they moved as a group towards the flapping tents.

All was quiet.

As they approached the camp, Zain suddenly started shouting, "Hallo! All hail!" and the others took up the cry. Then they ran at full pelt towards the tents, with Quinn trailing behind. He could only wonder in awe at the cohesion of the group – they'd clearly done this before.

Once in the camp, they began slicing through tents, quickly revealing their interiors. There would be no hiding. But there was no one to hide.

Congealing fish sat in a pan atop a black campfire. Zain poked the ashes with the tip of his sword. "Cold," he said. "Wherever they've gone, they went a while ago."

He looked up. "We spread out in pairs, and we look," he said. "Quinn, you're with me."

Quinn peered into the deep gloom of the forest of trees that began at the edge of the sand. His heart was racing. Was Ajax in there? With whom? How would they ever find them?

There was only one way to answer these questions. He started after Zain, who was already disappearing into the line of trees.

Chapter Seven

"*Are we there yet?*" Though he didn't voice the question, Quinn's legs asked it. Legs that had been at sea for weeks on end didn't much like being asked to perform long hikes within minutes of stepping on dry land. Quinn found he kept wandering sideways, off the path forged by Zain, who seemed tireless as he pounded ahead.

The trees around them were packed together like the scones his mam sometimes baked. Their thin trunks grew tall, branching out into a dark-green canopy high above their heads. The undergrowth was sparse, but their footsteps were muffled by a thick layer of rotting leaves. The air smelled damp and musky, and there was a constant skittering sound as small creatures found an urgent need to be elsewhere.

Idly, Quinn wondered if there were large creatures in these parts as well. He shuddered and hurried to follow Zain more closely.

"Do I look cold?" the Deslonder asked.

Given the sheen of sweat that coated the back of both their necks, this was a strange question.

"No," Quinn answered. "Why?"

"Get any closer and I'll be wearing you as a cloak," the Deslonder said. His words were stern, but Quinn thought he detected an undertone of amusement.

He blushed and moved back a step or two.

"I see a clearing up ahead," said Zain. "Quietly now."

Quinn barely breathed as they stole forward. Now that Zain pointed it out, he could see a lightening of the canopy ahead. They stuck closely to the cover afforded by the tree trunks, though the idea of Zain hiding behind one was laughable. He'd be lucky to get one arm hidden.

They crept to the edge of the clearing, secreting themselves behind a large rock. Where had it come from? Quinn hadn't seen any others like it in the woods.

Peering over the top, they saw that they'd happened upon some kind of village. But it was unlike any other that Quinn had ever seen. All the buildings, such as they were, were constructed of three tree trunks, tall and thin, propped together, with various animal hides – cow and goat mostly from what he could see – sewn together and wrapped around them. There was one very large central tent with smaller ones arranged around it in a circular pattern. Paths were cleared between the tents, gardens were planted outside them. At one end was a town square of some sort, with rows of logs arranged in front of a raised stage. At the other, simple pens constructed from wood held horses, cows and goats, while chickens and small, dark-haired children roamed free through the village. The children were dressed uniformly in fringed leather breeches and matching tunics.

Quinn stilled. When he'd pictured the other lands they might visit on the journey to map the world, he hadn't ever stopped to consider that there might be other people in them. Now, of course, he was kicking himself. If there were people in Verdania and different people in Gelyn and even more different people in Deslond, then why should there not be other people in other lands?

The question was, were they friendly?

Zain seemed to be asking himself the same question. There was no sign of Ajax, Odilon or the rest of the crew from the *Fair Maiden*. Did that mean they weren't here? Or were they hidden inside that large, main tent?

There was only one way to find out.

"Quinn, you need to sneak over there and have a look in that big tent," whispered Zain.

Him? Was *he* the one with a fierce reputation as a Deslond warrior?

"Um, I've never . . ."

"Don't tell me you've never snuck in anywhere you weren't wanted," said Zain.

"Of course I have," he answered. "But that was spying on my brother Simon when he was courting Merryn. Or avoiding Da when he wanted me to feed the pigs. Not creeping into a foreign village in a strange land."

"Same, same," said Zain. "Did you get caught those other times?"

Quinn hesitated. "No," he said, reluctantly.

"Then you know everything you need to know," said Zain. "If a girl being kissed when she shouldn't didn't know you were there, nobody will. Besides, you're of a much better size to be sneaking than I am."

Quinn gulped. He'd thought the scribe wasn't supposed to be put at risk! He considered reminding Zain that he needed him to create the map, as a last-ditch effort to remain behind the safety of the rock, but he was more afraid of the Deslonder's response than he was of whatever might be in that tent.

"It's a lot riskier to either sit here or to have me creeping about in there, trust me," Zain continued, as though Quinn had spoken. "If a frontal attack were required, I'm your man. Creeping isn't my strong point."

Again, Quinn heard that undertone of a smile. This time, it reassured him. If Zain were relaxed enough to make what, for him, was a sidesplitting joke, then he mustn't think there was much to fear.

Quinn stole out from behind the rock and began to make his way slowly, fading from tree trunk to tree trunk, to the edge of the clearing. There was no sign of any adult movement in the camp, though he could see campfire smoke and smell delicious things cooking, and the children were all absorbed in a game near the animal pens.

He considered his next move. His clothing was different from what the children were wearing, but he and Aysha had often discovered that the simplest way to avoid detection in any situation was to look as though you belonged. So you didn't try to creep away from the plowing fields, you simply picked up the nearest sheaf of wheat and walked off with it, looking as though you had somewhere to be.

He wondered if it worked in reverse. He could only hope.

He stepped out into the open, waiting for a startled cry or alert to be sounded. There was nothing. Not taking too many chances, he tried to stay as close to the tents as possible, ducking behind the nearest cover, waiting for a minute to see if anyone had noticed him, and moving only when he was certain the coast was clear.

He had time in several places to take note of the plants in the gardens at his feet – he'd never seen the tiny, bright-red fruit before, but they were obviously a staple food source in this village. Strange – in nature, red was usually a warning not to eat.

By the time he reached the main tent, he was sweating even more, feeling it run in rivulets down his sides. He put his ear to the goat hide, listening hard. Inside, he could hear a hum of conversation, none of it recognizable.

Then he heard one voice, louder than the rest.

"You must let us go. We mean you no harm. We are simply racing around the world."

Odilon!

A babble of voices met this plea. None of them sounded particularly friendly.

Quinn looked around quickly. All was still quiet. Dropping to the ground, he pulled the knife from his boot and used it to cut a slit at eye level in the hide lining of the tent. Pulling the slit open, he was able to see inside – at boot level, anyway. As it turned out, boot level was what was required.

The interior of the tent was larger than he'd imagined from its outside appearance. It was dim, but not dark, thanks to the daylight pouring in through the entrance flap, which had been left open. He thanked the stars that he'd approached from this side, which appeared to be the rear of the tent.

There were about twenty people in the tent, all men, and all uniformly dressed in loose hide outfits, similar to what the children outside were wearing. Their hair, ranging in color from midnight black to silver gray, was long, either held in place with a leather thong around the forehead, or braided loosely at the back. Their faces were painted with elaborate stripes in brilliant colors – red, white, ocher, black. A haze of smoke shimmered above their heads.

At the center of the circle, back to back and lashed tightly to the tent's sturdy center pole, was Ajax, Odilon and six other members of their crew. Quinn frowned. He'd been sure that the larger ship had a crew of eight. Where were the other two?

Even as the thought struck him, the men in the room began to chant, voices rising in unison, the speed building with each word. The eight Verdanians looked terrified. They'd clearly heard this chant before, and it didn't bode well.

Quinn sat up. He'd heard enough. It was time to go back to Zain, find the others, and pull out that full-frontal attack the Deslonder had mentioned earlier. He jumped to his feet in one easy motion, turned on his heel and – ran straight into a solid chest. A solid bare chest.

This could not be good.

The man, long dark hair flowing behind him, grabbed Quinn on the shoulder. Reflexively, Quinn brought his shoulder forward in one quick action, loosening the man's grasp. The man bellowed, lunging for Quinn again. Quinn ducked under his arm, sidestepping quickly, and brought his left leg around in a sweeping motion. At the same time, he grabbed the man's outstretched arm, pulling, and knocking his foot out from under him. The man went down hard and Quinn ran – mentally thanking Zain for all those early morning training sessions. He was right. Practicing the movements over and over had made them instinctive.

Looking neither left nor right, Quinn raced through the camp, hearing the cries of the man behind him – and then the cries of many others as they gathered together and gave chase. He ran faster. It was amazing how fear gave you speed you never thought you had.

He bolted towards the rock, flinging himself behind it, dragging breath into his lungs. "Ajax. Odilon. Big tent. Tied up," he managed.

"Good to see you haven't lost your ability to creep unnoticed," Zain said wryly. "How many in the camp?"

"Saw. About. Twenty. Men," gasped Quinn. He wasn't sure if it was the run or the idea of twenty of those fearsome men chasing him that forced the breath from his chest.

Zain nodded, raised his head and whistled three times. Quinn knew that call. The blue-crested whipbird, native to Verdania. "The others will be here as soon as they can," said Zain. "In the meantime, get that kitchen knife out of your boot and follow me."

Quinn felt the blood leave his head. "We're going back in there?" He could hear the ferocious pack of men thundering their way, calling to each other.

Zain nodded. "We are. But we'll only fight if we have to."

Okay, thought Quinn, failing to see quite how the Deslonder was going to avoid a battle.

"Words are always best, Quinn," Zain said. "Only fight if you have to."

Quinn shook his head with disbelief, but leaned down to extract the kitchen knife. Zain drew his mighty sword, looked back at Quinn and nodded.

Then he was gone, yelling loud enough to make noise for ten men, and all Quinn could do was follow.

The dark-haired men rounded the nearest tent, armed with clubs and sticks, just as Zain burst into the clearing at full speed, still yelling, huge sword flashing in the sun as he swung it around his head. Quinn held his knife in front of him, point up, snarling as best he could, and stayed as close to his captain as he could without getting in the way of that swirling sword.

The pack stopped dead, openmouthed. It was clear they'd never seen anyone quite like Zain before. Then again, thought Quinn, few had. They all looked at each other, uncertain, as Zain continued to yell and shout and wave his sword about. Muttering broke out amongst the men, and Quinn, still keeping up his own snarling and carrying on, could see that they were trying to work out what to do next.

Suddenly Zain stopped shouting, though his sword remained poised. A few seconds later, Quinn also let his voice die away. Silence settled over the clearing.

Zain bowed his head slightly. "I am Zain," he said.

The men looked at each other, and then an older man, hair streaked with silver, stepped forward. He was wearing a chain around his neck that seemed to be fashioned from teeth that were as long as Quinn's fingers. Quinn shuddered when he saw it, unable to imagine a beast so huge.

The man inclined his head. "Adahy," he said, striking his chest.

Quinn was aware of the other Verdanian crew members materializing around him and immediately felt better. They were still outnumbered more than two to one, but at least they were together.

The man was speaking again. The language was unlike anything Quinn had heard before. He listened hard. He had taught himself to speak Renz in two days the previous summer because he'd wanted to read a particular book that Cleric Redland had told his mother about. When a traveling merchant from Firenze had arrived in Markham with his wife Maree, he'd asked her for help. She had laughed when he'd asked her to walk him around the village, pointing to everything and giving him the Renz word for it, but she'd humored him to the point of speaking only Renz to him when he'd asked. It had made for a strange few days for her, but he'd simply filed all the words away in his memory. By the time she left, he'd picked up enough to get the book from Cleric Redland and work out the rest from context. And Maree was none the wiser as to just how much she'd taught him.

Learning Renz had given him a taste for languages and he'd sought out books to help. He'd started with Suspite, the language at the heart of all languages, mostly used for trade, and this had helped him to figure out the basics of Gelynion, and even a little Athelstanish. He was also making good progress with Deslondic – though only Zain knew about that, and only by accident.

He'd been sitting in the wheelhouse one morning, checking navigation charts with Zain, when Cleaver had come in and told Zain, in Deslondic, that he'd noticed a change in the coastline. Without thinking, Quinn had made a note of the change on the chart. Cleaver hadn't noticed – but Zain didn't miss it.

"So," he said. "You understand our language."

"Er, just a little," said Quinn, kicking himself. "Just what I've, er, picked up."

"Hmm," was the only response, but Quinn noticed that Zain went out of his way from then on to add to Quinn's knowledge of the language where he could.

But all of those languages used the same alphabet and sounds as Verdanian – while this one seemed to have little in common.

Zain and Adahy were still staring at each other. Zain lowered his sword, gesturing for the crew to do the same.

Quinn noted that he kept his grip tight on the sword, so he lowered his knife and did the same.

Adahy nodded, motioning for his side to lower their weapons. The men warily obeyed, though Quinn noticed several fingering their clubs impatiently.

Zain stepped forward. "Friends," he said, pointing at the crew, and smiling. Quinn thought that now wasn't the time to let the Deslonder know that he should show fewer teeth when he was trying to convince someone of his friendly nature . . .

Adahy cocked his head. It was clear that he had no idea what Zain was on about.

Zain grabbed Quinn, dragging him forward, and gathering him up into a bear hug. "Friends," he repeated.

Quinn, gasping for breath as the big man squeezed him, said, "You might want to be a bit gentler – they'll think we want to squash them."

Adahy laughed, apparently enjoying the image. He nodded, pointed to his men, and said a word in his language that Quinn took to mean friends.

Taking quick advantage of the opening, Zain pointed to the big central tent. "Friends," he said.

Adahy stopped laughing. He shook his head and proceeded to deliver a torrent of words, not one of which any of them understood.

Zain and Quinn looked at each other. "Those language skills of yours . . ." Zain began.

"Are about to be tested, I'd imagine," Quinn answered, as calmly as possible.

"Yes," said Zain, no sign of humor in his voice. "And failure is not an option. Not unless you want us all to die."

Chapter Eight

Ash was bored. She'd been on the ship with Cleric Greenfield for the better part of two days now and couldn't face another game of chip and dice. Even now, the cleric was below decks setting up the board, carefully placing his six white chips in a row. Much as she liked the old man, with his gentle eyes and wide knowledge of herbs and flowers, Ash thought she might scream. Surely Zain and the others should have returned by now? It had been yesterday morning when they'd disappeared into the trees.

Before he'd left, Zain had given her a list of instructions. Number one: under no circumstances was she to leave the ship. Number two: she was not to leave the ship. Number three: she had to stay on board no matter what.

But surely he hadn't been expecting this? After all, what was she to do without him and the crew? Sail Cleric Greenfield home across the ocean by herself? Somewhere in the back of her mind was a nasty little voice that kept telling her they were all dead and that she was alone on a ship with an old man in the middle of nowhere.

But it never did any good to listen to nasty little voices like that.

Besides, she couldn't believe that Quinn was dead. They were practically related. Surely she'd feel it. Like she had when her mam had died. They hadn't had to tell her. She'd felt it deep inside, a small gasp, like a light had been extinguished. Even now, remembering that awful feeling brought tears to her eyes.

She wiped them away furiously. It wouldn't do to give way to girlish tears now. She had a job to do.

She went below to check on Cleric Greenfield. Deep, rhythmic snores greeted her before she'd even left the deck. She had no idea how Quinn or Zain slept down here at night – the cleric snored loud enough to wake the fish. Clearly the exertion of setting up the board had been too much for him, and he'd dropped off for his regular afternoon nap.

She went back up on deck to check the position of the sun. Three o'clock. She had at least two hours before the cleric even woke up, looking for his supper. She'd be well gone by then.

The question was, how was she going to go? The crew had taken the longboat – she could see it, still pulled up on the beach, slightly to the right of the camp. She had only one alternative. She would have to swim. She swallowed, her throat suddenly dry, measuring the distance to the beach. At least as long as Farmer Freeman's wheat field, which was, she knew, about fifty paces. She was a strong swimmer, but that was in the river at home, which was only thirty paces across, and was flat, and not too deep. She couldn't even see the bottom of the ocean here, and she knew that Zain's lead-weight line had run out a long way in its search for depth.

Still, she had to do something. If Zain and the crew didn't come back, she and Cleric Greenfield would be marooned. If she couldn't swim to shore, what luck would she have trying to get the good cleric there?

She looked down at herself. The leather breeches she was wearing would hold water. She needed something lighter. Rummaging around in the wheelhouse, she unearthed the long johns she'd worn during the ocean crossing, before they'd seen that monstrous beast and the weather had changed for the better.

It felt strange to be walking about on deck clad in only underwear, but she knew she would be thankful for the lack of fabric once she was in the water. She wished she had her kitchen knife, but she'd given it to Quinn – and besides, where would she put it? Smiling to herself, she walked to the rope ladder dangling over the side of the ship. With any luck, she'd find a knife in the camp – along with a pair of breeches.

Within seconds, she was over the side and making her way down the wooden hull to the water below. Reaching it, she dangled one foot in the brine, hanging off the ladder with one hand. She could still stay here. Even as the inviting thought danced across her mind, she heard faint cries from the trees, carried to her on the light breeze.

She frowned, cocking her head and listening hard, but there was nothing more than the lapping of water against the hull. Closing her mind to any thoughts of staying on board – and any doubts about what might be lurking below the benign surface of the water – she took a deep breath and dived in, setting a course for the longboat.

At least, whichever way things went, she wouldn't have to swim back.

~

Quinn's head hurt. The constant hubbub of chatter in the tent, the permanent haze of smoke, a lack of sleep and the effort of concentrating intensely for more than a whole day were beginning to take a toll on him. He could feel Zain watching him closely, but he resisted the temptation to look over at his captain. It would only make him miserable to see Zain, Jericho, Abel and the rest of the crew lashed beside Ajax, Odilon and the others, with the ropes stolen from the *Fair Maiden*.

Still, he had a job to do. Surrounded by local warriors, Zain had given the *Libertas* crew word that they were to allow themselves to be captured. Shaking their heads, they'd gone along with it. And so had Quinn, with Zain's words about language ringing in his ears.

So he'd *used* his ears, listening hard to the warriors around him, looking for repetition of sounds and phrases. Knowing that their prisoners could not understand them, the warriors spoke freely as they herded the *Libertas* crew into the large tent, stripped them of their weapons, and tied them next to the other Verdanians.

Odilon had made his distaste at having to sit with slaves quite obvious the moment Zain had been brought into the tent.

"Is it not enough that we are tied like common criminals?" he protested. "Now we are to be treated like slaves as well?"

Ajax, who had brightened up visibly at their entrance, had hissed at his captain, "Master Odilon, they may be our only chance out of here."

"Hmph," grunted the nobleman. "I fail to see how, when they're tied up next to us."

Quinn wanted to tell the man to shut up, that Zain had only ended up in this mess because they were trying to rescue *him*. But Zain had seemed to sense his anguish and stilled him with an almost imperceptible shake of the head.

So Quinn had concentrated on the task at hand and was soon picking up words. He had no idea what they meant, but it didn't take long before he had enough to begin parroting them, under his breath, every time one of their captors came anywhere near him – a fact that had caused great consternation in the warriors. He had a feeling that most of what he was saying wasn't complimentary . . .

Adahy was fetched and Quinn, heart skittering around in his chest, sure he was about to be killed, was dragged off, to the horror of the other Verdanians (bar Odilon). But the older man seemed more interested in studying him and, for the first time in his life, Quinn was happy to display the full extent of what he could do. His freakish memory was going to either give him the skills to talk them all out of this or, at the very least, buy them time to plan an escape.

Which was why he was currently cloistered away to one side of the tent with an old man draped in beads and feathers, while Adahy watched on. The old man, named Otenu, was teaching him the local language – and Quinn was absorbing it as fast as he could. He could see the other Verdanians, quiet now and exhausted from struggling and shouting, sending him puzzled glances, but he was confident that none were close enough to actually hear what was going on. He had to hope that, if he did convince Adahy to let him try to plead their case publicly, Zain would be able to convince the other Verdanians that the freakish display wasn't something to be scared of.

But he'd worry about that if they all survived.

At times he and Otenu left the tent, accompanied by two fierce-looking warriors who carried clubs. Quinn took the opportunity during these outings, when Otenu, who seemed to be the village healer, took him through the maze of tents and gardens, to take in as much of the layout as he could, along with the words the man was trying to teach him. He wasn't sure which was going to be more useful – the words to talk their way out, or the layout to fight their way out – but he was hedging his bets.

And now the time had come to discover which it would be.

Quinn took a sip of water from the leather pouch he'd been given. His throat was dry, the pounding in his head was growing worse, and he was feeling altogether sorry for himself. But it was time for his make-or-break performance.

Adahy had been surprised when Quinn had told him what he wanted to do, but had, after discussion with Otenu and other elders, agreed.

Silence fell on the tent as Adahy stood.

"This boy will now speak," he told the locals in his own language. "He will plead the case for release of the prisoners, and you will understand him."

The crowd laughed in astonishment and insults were shouted from every corner. Quinn breathed a sigh of relief. He'd understood every word so far.

"You will give him fair hearing," Adahy continued, breaking through the ridicule. "Chances are this will be over in seconds and then we can continue the sacrifice at Big Rock."

Quinn swallowed hard. They were all to be killed if he couldn't pull this off. The use of the word "continue" also gave him pause. He remembered the missing crewmen from the *Fair Maiden*. And the rock behind which Zain and he had hidden . . .

He became aware of a deepening silence and the fact that all eyes were upon him. His eyes sought Zain's. The Deslonder winked.

Quinn almost smiled. Almost. Only Zain could wink under circumstances such as these. Then again, Quinn thought, perhaps he'd been in worse predicaments. It was a comforting thought.

He stood, gathering his thoughts, running through the file of pictures in his mind on which the local language was painted. He didn't pray much – his family tended to put their faith more in the seasons and nature than in any particular god, though Verdania did offer many to choose from – but he directed a few quiet words to any benevolent higher being who might be listening.

And then he began to speak.

~

Ash shivered as the sun began to dip below the horizon. Pulling the large man-sized tunic she'd found in Odilon's camp closer around her, she began to regret her decision not to remove the long johns as well. When the tunic was all she'd been able to find to cover herself, the idea of taking off her underwear had seemed immodest. Now that the sun's drying rays were disappearing, though, she wondered whether half-naked might not have been better than half-frozen.

At least she'd managed to find this village – if that's what you'd call it, she thought, looking at the strange structures around her – before darkness fell. It seemed deserted and she wondered if everyone was simply tucked up for the night, or if she should be worried about something more sinister.

When she'd seen the state of the camp on the beach, she'd followed her instinct and the path that Zain had taken through the trees. Fortunately, being such a large man, he'd left a clear trail through the leafy debris on the forest floor, and she could see the smaller, lighter steps of Quinn as well. They'd led her straight to a large rock set near this clearing. Now all she had to do was to see if they were still here.

Moving as quietly as possible, she picked her way through the tents until she reached the largest one in the center. There were no voices from within, though she thought she could hear movement. She pressed her ear to the hide-covered wall and listened hard.

Now there was one voice. A young male. Speaking a language that she couldn't understand. She needed to hear better.

Scanning the tent wall, she noticed a slit cut into the hide down towards the bottom. Right where someone might have lain as they tried to see what was inside. She was on her stomach in a trice, peering into the tent.

Quinn!

She couldn't believe her eyes. He was standing in the center of the tent, addressing a huge group of people. At least she thought they were people. With their painted faces they could have been the demons from the stories that her mother had told her. But Quinn was speaking to them. He wouldn't speak to demons.

She couldn't believe her eyes as his mouth opened and a river of words streamed out. A singsong, foreign river. What was he saying?

Before she could think any more of it, she became aware of a pair of eyes staring directly at the hole she was looking through. Large, dark eyes set in a large, dark face. Zain! She blinked slowly to show that she'd seen him and he blinked back.

Quinn was still speaking and all other eyes in the tent were on him, so Ash felt brave enough to rip the hide a little wider, so that Zain could see more than one eye. His own eyes widened as he recognized her, and he frowned.

She had a feeling he'd have a few words to say to her once all this was over.

In the meantime, though, she was the only one outside the tent. She could see the strong rope that held Zain and the others tight. She needed to do something about it while all the attention was on Quinn. But what? More than ever she wished she hadn't given Quinn that kitchen knife.

Kitchen! That was it. Where there was a kitchen there would be a cutting implement of some kind. And she needed to get one to Zain so that he could get out of those ropes.

She rolled away from the hole, coming up onto all fours to look around. Still no one. With any luck, the entire village was in the large tent, leaving the coast clear.

In the deepening twilight she roamed from one nearby tent to another, without finding anything that suggested a kitchen. Frustration growing, she widened her search, passing several gardens in the process. The plant woman in her wanted to stop and examine each one closely, particularly the tall plants that the tribe had tied to stakes, some bearing clusters of round, bright-red fruit. What could they be? The only red fruit eaten in Verdania were the redenberries that grew wild in the hedgerows. Everything else with a pretty rouge blush was known to induce a very unattractive death. And yet, the people here were tending these. Were they medicinal only? Judging by the numbers of them, she thought not. Only edible plants were grown in that quantity.

She was getting farther and farther from the central tent and still hadn't found anything vaguely useful for cutting when she stumbled, literally, upon the amphitheater that marked the top end of the village. The stage had been decorated with strings of feathers, and more feathers adorned the tall pole at its center. She shivered, this time not from the cool night air on her damp skin. It was clear that there was to be some kind of ceremony here – and she didn't like the fat ropes looping that pole.

Then she spied the basket set to one side of the stage. In it she could see several sticks, also adorned in feathers. Could there be something useful there?

She scrambled across the stone benches and, somewhat belatedly, looked hurriedly around to see if she was being observed. There was no one in sight. Even so, she dropped to a crouch and crept up onto the stage, pulling the basket down beside her to examine its contents.

There were half a dozen or so of the hollow sticks, each with feathers tied to one end. The other end was tipped with a sharp, pointed rock. Arrows! Was there a bow nearby? She searched the confines of the stage, but there was nothing. She took three of the arrows anyway, reasoning that the sharp tip might come in handy. As she pulled them out, she noticed a gleam in the bottom of the basket. Reaching in carefully to avoid cutting herself on the remaining arrows, she pushed them aside to reveal a wicked-looking, curved-blade knife lying in the bottom. It too was adorned with feathers. But why would anyone need a knife with such a sickle-like blade?

Shrugging, she grabbed the knife by its leather-wrapped handle. Zain would know what to do with it. Then, as quickly as she could without losing her precious cargo – or doing herself damage – she ran back to the tent.

~

Inside, Quinn was sweating. The heat in the room, produced by so many bodies packed into it, was rising even as the sun dropped like a stone outside. He had been speaking now for fifteen minutes, aware that the longer he could talk – and still make sense – the more difficult it would be for Adahy to back out of the deal. He had spoken at length about the race – struggling to find the right words to explain the map or the world. He could see the confusion on the faces of the people in front of him. People who could have no concept of the scale of the ocean they'd just crossed.

He had heard them speaking as he'd taken his place in the circle. They had no idea just how much he'd gleaned from his one day of lessons and so had no qualms about talking openly amongst themselves about the gold they'd stolen from Odilon's ship. Or how they planned to use both ships to attack their own neighbors down the coast. Once they'd sacrificed the Verdanians, that was.

His only hope was to bewitch them with their own language. And he'd done his best.

They'd gasped when he first began speaking. Yes, he'd stuttered a little, throwing his arms around as though to grab the right words out of the air. But he managed to put enough together to be understood. And he gained confidence as he spoke.

Out of the corner of his eye, he could see the other Verdanians staring at him. Only Zain was not in shock. He was facing the back of the tent, but Quinn could tell by his relaxed posture that he was unfazed by Quinn's feat. In fact, if Quinn didn't know differently, he'd swear Zain's attention was altogether somewhere else.

He was nearing the end of his little speech, talking about how they came in peace, and would leave in peace, when a man near the doorway suddenly stood, pointed directly at him and began shouting. At first Quinn tried to continue, but the man simply shouted louder. So Quinn stopped speaking and listened. The man, tall, strong and painted all over in stripes of red and yellow, stamped his feet and gesticulated wildly, causing the chest piece he was wearing, made of feathers and bones, Quinn noted, to clink together.

He was accusing Quinn of being some kind of devil.

Quinn shifted nervously from foot to foot, heart racing. He remembered the rocks thrown at Aysha's mam. He licked his lips, mouth dry, glancing over at Zain for support. But Zain was staring fixedly at a spot where the wooden tent pole nearest him met the ground.

"This is black magic!" the warrior was shouting. "They are demons. There is no peace with these people, only death and destruction."

Adahy held his hands up for peace, but the mumbling that had begun when the warrior started speaking gathered pace and volume, until the tent buzzed like a hive of angry wasps.

Quinn tried again. "I'm not a devil – just a quick learner," he said desperately, voice shaking, but his words fell on deaf ears. So much for Zain's notion about words being the first course of action, he thought, terror rising. They were going to have to fight their way out of here if they were going to leave alive – and thirteen of them were bound together with thick rope, useless.

Behind him, the Verdanians were also muttering. Quinn could hear Odilon's angry voice, and Ajax trying to placate him.

And then he heard Zain. The Deslonder's voice rose above the din in a huge bellow and as his voice rose, so did his body. He was standing, tearing at the ropes that bound him, dragging the other Verdanians to their feet.

The locals were startled into silence and it was that pause that gave the Verdanians the chink they needed. Grabbing whatever was to hand – clubs, crockery, the rope itself – they began fighting their way through the crowd. Their task was made easier by the fact that many of the locals, terrified by the devil boy who spoke their tongue and the huge black demon who'd broken free of thick ropes, simply melted away, disappearing under the tent walls to safety, dragging women and children with them.

Only the warriors remained, the twenty or so that Quinn and Zain had faced alone the day before. But the fight was a lot more even with the *Fair Maiden* crew involved – and Zain seemed to relish the prospect.

"Take Ajax and Ash and get down to the longboat," said Zain, even as he took hold of one dark-haired local who had foolishly rushed him. Using the man's momentum, Zain flipped him up and over his shoulder with the ease of years of practice. The man landed with a sickening thud.

"Ash?" said Quinn, watching openmouthed.

"Now's not the time for conversation," grunted Zain, turning suddenly to smash a long-haired warrior in the face, using his braid to pull him close and then swinging him into the dirt behind him. Right at Quinn's feet. "She's here. She got the knife that got us free."

How had she managed that?

"What knife?" Quinn asked, just as he was grabbed from behind. At first he froze, but then his training kicked in and he slumped forward to loosen the man's grip. Caught off balance, the man fell and Quinn used the man's own weight to pull him over his head and onto his back – on top of his comrade.

Zain nodded approvingly, before pulling a huge, curved knife from behind his back and holding it aloft.

"This one," he said. "The one they were planning to use on us later to cut us up for their gods."

At the sight of the blade, the teeming mass of warriors paused again, casting anguished glances at each other. It was obviously important to them.

"I don't think they're happy," noted Quinn.

"I'm not interested in their emotional state – I just want to get out of here in one piece and I want you to follow orders. Get your friends and go!"

The force on the last word was enough to convince Quinn. Ducking through the brawling crowd, he spotted Ajax's bright hair in a corner, where he was wrestling with a local boy about his own age. Ajax had the size advantage, but the boy was a wily fighter and had the benefit of a short spear in his hand. Ajax was fending him off with a large wooden serving platter.

Quinn rushed to help his friend, but before he got there, Ison crept up behind the long-haired local and crumpled him at the knees with a well-placed kick. Ajax caught him, delivered a crushing punch to his jaw, and then laid him down gently on the floor of the tent, like a sleeping baby.

"Thanks for that," he said to Ison, who grinned. "I wasn't sure how much longer that platter would hold out."

"We have to go," said Quinn to Ajax, as he bent to pick up the discarded spear. As he did so, Quinn noticed a large, sharp tooth in the dirt nearby. It was like those he'd seen on Adahy's necklace, which must have been broken in a fight. Quinn picked it up and put it in his pocket.

"This way!" he shouted, heading for the side of the tent, where he used the spear to rip a long gash down it – and then handed the spear to Ison. "You've probably got more use for this than we do." Ison took it and threw himself back into the melee.

"Aw, do we have to?" Ajax said, watching him go, and looking bereft at the idea of missing the fight.

"Zain's given us a job," said Quinn. "We have to go."

Ajax nodded. His short time with the Deslonder had told him everything he needed to know about Zain's leadership skills – and expectations. Even tied to a pole, Zain was calm and in control. Which was more than could be said for Odilon, whose peevish whining had tested everybody's nerves.

Ajax followed Quinn outside, eyes adjusting to the dark as the din in the tent grew louder. "Which way?" he asked.

"To the beach," said Quinn. "We need to get the boat

ready to head back to the ship. In a hurry. But first . . . Ash! . . . Ash!"

His urgent calls weren't answered. Then, seconds later, she appeared next to him, arms full of plants and bowls, barefoot.

"Where are your shoes?" he demanded. "How can we get back in the dark without them?"

"Same way I got here," she said. "I couldn't swim in them. I had to leave them behind."

Swim? He shook his head. There were clearly stories to be told but they would need to wait.

"Come on," he said. "Back to the boat. What in the world have you got there?"

He waved his hand at her armload. "I don't know," she said. "I want to take a closer look. You carry these." She handed three earthenware bowls, which Quinn could now see were full of soil, to Ajax.

"Why do we need these?" the redhead asked, struggling to balance them. "Are we going to throw them?"

"They're to keep the plants in," she said, an unspoken "you numbskull" ringing in the air between them. Fortunately, Ajax merely grinned again and the three of them raced towards the large rock, their only landmark in the walls of trees around them – all of which looked alike.

Once they got to the rock, Quinn listened hard for the waves crashing on the beach and ran that way, the others following. He could only hope that Zain wouldn't be too far behind.

~

"Where's your longboat?" Quinn asked Ajax as they finally reached the shore. They could see the hulking shadows of the two ships looming in the bay. So near and yet so far.

"They took it," said Ajax. "We'd only been on shore about two hours. They waited till we settled in and then rushed in, screaming and yelling, and overwhelmed us."

"That must have been scary," said Ash.

Ajax mustered up as much dignity as he could manage. "It was," he said shortly.

"What happened on the ship?"

"They'd already been there," said Ajax, bitterly. "We didn't even notice. Odilon was so adamant that we eat straightaway and by the time we'd put up the camp . . . They went in off those rocks over there." He indicated an outcrop on the left-hand side of the bay.

"Killed the lookouts and took the ropes – and the door handles." His voice rose a little in amazement at that fact. "We were in all sorts of trouble before you turned up."

Quinn was too busy to even acknowledge the compliment. He was trying to work out how they were going to get fifteen people into a longboat made for eight without sinking it.

He gave up. Ash had swum in, they'd swim back if they had to.

"Push the boat down to the water," he said. "Grab what you can from the supplies. I'm afraid you're going to be without a longboat from now on."

"That's okay," said Ajax. "We've another. Nothing but the best for Odilon."

Quinn's jaw dropped. How had he missed that on his visit to the *Fair Maiden*?

"It's covered up, in the stern," said Ajax, as though he'd read Quinn's thoughts.

"Right – can you swim?"

"Can I . . . swim?" asked Ajax.

Ash groaned. "Not again," she said. "I only just made it the first time. Though the *Fair Maiden* is a lot closer."

Quinn managed a laugh. "No," he said. "You stay here. Keep the boat at the water's edge, ready for action. Ajax and I are going to swim out to the *Fair Maiden* as fast as we can and bring that boat back."

"We are?" questioned Ajax.

But Quinn was already removing his boots, throwing them in the longboat, along with his breeches and his tunic. Clad only in drawers, he was soon wading through the surf. Ajax could do nothing but follow.

Ash watched anxiously from the shore as the two boys swam through the dark water towards the *Fair Maiden*. A light breeze had sprung up, lifting the hairs on her arms, though she was long past the point where she was cold. The huge moon slipped from behind a cloud, bringing light to the beach, and she breathed a sigh of relief as she saw two heads surface near the ship's rope ladder. Within seconds they were climbing up the ladder, and minutes later she saw the longboat being lowered on ropes from the stern.

Behind her, in the trees, she could hear shouts. Getting closer. And closer. She shivered with fear. If the local warriors found her here, alone on the beach, she couldn't even imagine what might happen to her. She sat on the edge of the boat, poised for action, her plants nestled under a seat inside.

She could hear the rhythmic splash of oars as the other longboat was rowed towards the shore. Ajax had taken both the oars and was rowing like a boy possessed. At the same time, she could hear running feet, and bodies thrashing through the trees.

Two men hurtled out of the trees and onto the beach. To her relief, it was Odilon and one of his crew, not the local warriors. "Over here!" she shouted. They pelted down the beach to her, throwing themselves into the boat, completely out of breath.

"Row!" commanded Odilon.

"What?" Ash was stunned. He was going to leave them all behind. He knew nothing of the other boat on its way, hadn't even glanced in that direction. After all that Zain and the others had done for him, he would leave them to their fate?

"Row!" shouted the nobleman. "Are you deaf, boy?"

Of course, he thought she was a boy.

She shook her head. "I'm not rowing. The others are coming."

"Curse you!" said Odilon, sitting up and grasping an oar. "You don't know they're coming. We need to get out of here! Alphonse, grab that oar."

His crew member looked dumbfounded under his beard. "But what about Jeremiah, and the others?" he said, naming his first mate.

"We'll all die if we sit here," screamed Odilon, eyes wide with panic.

"Here they come!" shouted Alphonse, with relief. And it was true, Odilon's crew was sprinting across the sand towards them.

"Get in! Get in!" shouted Odilon. "Row!"

And two of the men picked up oars as the others began to push off.

"Wait!" shrieked Ash. "We can't leave the others! Zain!"

"A slave," said Odilon with contempt. "You would lose your life for a slave."

"He risked his life for you!" she screamed at him.

"Bah!" said Odilon, "I would have worked something out."

"Yeah, right," said Ash, grabbing her plants and bowls and scrambling out of the boat.

"What are you doing, you stupid boy?"

"Getting out," she said. "I'll wait for the next one."

"Ha!" he screamed. "Stay and die then." And with that, the two rowers began to pull and the boat moved quickly through the waves.

Pounding feet behind her dragged her attention back to the sand. Zain, Jericho, Abel and the other crew members from the *Libertas*! Zain was dragging his heavy sword, as well as the curved ceremonial knife, while Jericho had taken possession of a large spear, and Ison a small one.

"Where's the boat?" shouted Zain as he neared. "They're right behind us."

"Here it is!" shouted a voice behind Ash. With three huge pulls, Ajax launched the boat onto a wave and surfed into the shore, Quinn grinning in the bow. The crew piled in, and Jericho and Cleaver took over the rowing, pulling away from the shore in seconds. They were more than halfway to the *Fair Maiden* before everyone was breathing normally again, and it was about that time that the local warriors began to appear on the shore. Quinn gave them a jaunty wave as they shouted from the beach, shooting arrows that flew harmlessly into the black water near the boat.

They passed the *Fair Maiden*, and its crew had already

begun to unfurl the sails, the rope ladder and the longboat pulled up behind them.

"Do you think he's noticed I'm missing?" asked Ajax, watching, a combination of hope and fear in his voice.

Quinn wasn't sure how to answer. From what Ash had said, in his blind panic, Odilon probably hadn't. Given his comments about Zain, though, he wasn't sure.

"He's going to be very sad when he does," said Zain, from behind them. "Hard to win the race without a mapmaker."

There was a pause. "Which direction is he headed?" Zain asked Ajax.

"North," replied the redhead.

"Well, then, I can't see any harm in keeping him in suspense a little longer," said Zain, with a smile. "You stay with us for a few days. We're bound to catch up with him sooner or later."

They all laughed. Quinn could only imagine the competitive nobleman's reaction when he realized his prized mapmaker was missing – and, for all he knew, dead. As Zain had said, it was impossible to win the race without him.

As the longboat slid slowly but surely back to the *Libertas*, Quinn couldn't help but smile. He never thought he'd be so happy to see the ship!

It was funny how quickly a person's notion of home could change.

Chapter Nine

Quinn shivered and drew his cloak closer to his body. The deck bucked and rolled under him as the ship plunged down the face of another gigantic wave. Even in the confines of the wheelhouse he could feel the sea spray. The ocean was boiling with rage under gray, gloomy skies and mist covered the coastline, somewhere off the port side.

He stretched his fingers, trying to unfreeze them, and turned back to his task. It would probably be easier to be down in his watertight cabin, but he hated being in an airless, confined space when the seas were rough. Better to be on deck where the air was fresh, if bracing.

He was making good progress with his calculations and the sketch he was drawing of the coastline they were following. He couldn't draw anything to scale, of course, because he had no idea just how big that coastline might turn out to be, but he was using his journal to keep notes of distances, as best he could figure them. He'd also taken to keeping records on the walls of his cabin, all the better to preserve his precious supply of vellum.

Ash shrieked down near the bow as the ship hit the bottom of the trough and began the climb up the face of the wave, water showering over the cozy little nook beside the longboat where she and Ajax were sitting. Quinn looked down and shook his head. He'd yet to see Ajax do a shred of work on his map, though his friend had done some lightning quick sketches of the warriors at their last stop, capturing their essence in a few strokes. Quinn wasn't so sure he needed such a graphic reminder on his cabin walls, but he had to admit they were good.

"Well, I can't do much, can I?" the redhead had said with an easy grin, when Quinn had asked about his map. "Odilon has all my gear."

"Won't you have a big gap?" Quinn asked.

"Serves him right, doesn't it?" He paused as Quinn frowned. "Don't fret. It'll be okay," he continued. "There's not much here anyway, is there?"

It was true. The sheer granite cliffs had continued for a day or two, and had flattened out to a less dramatic but equally rocky landscape. Now the trees were few and far between, and they'd seen no sign of people of any kind. Coves and bays were also in short supply, but Quinn had dutifully noted the location of anything of any size on his cabin wall.

He glanced up from his calculations. The sky had grown even darker, and he knew they were in for another of the blustery tempests that hit them every five or six hours. Briefly he wondered if it was a warning from the gods, not to sail any farther. The end of the earth would be a bleak, desolate and stormy place, he imagined. All that water had to go somewhere.

He sighed, giving up for the day. He'd go down and join the others. If nothing else, it would be warmer tucked into that corner with the other two. In the past four days there'd been no sign of Odilon's ship and Ajax had made himself at home on board, joining in enthusiastically at the morning training sessions. To no one's surprise, he turned out to have a natural talent for the combat techniques, and was soon taking on the more seasoned crewmen in sparring bouts.

He was sharing Quinn's cabin, the pair talking long into the night about their journeys so far. When Quinn mentioned the Great White Beast, Ajax had sat straight up in his bed roll.

"We saw it too! Odilon was scared stiff. Thought it was a bad sign – didn't you?"

Quinn laughed. "We didn't know what to think. Still don't. But we've had good luck since, so maybe –"

"You call being captured good luck?"

"Well, technically, it was you lot who were captured," said Quinn. "We were playing out a strategy."

Ajax harumphed, lying down again. "Some strategy. If it hadn't been for Ash, we'd all be burned bread right now."

Quinn laughed. "Maybe so. I prefer to think of it as a team effort."

He had lain in the dark, listening as the other boy's breathing slowed and deepened. He didn't want to think too much about what might have happened if Ash hadn't turned up with that knife, but he liked to think that Zain had a backup plan. He'd only dared to ask him once, in a quiet moment, a few nights after their escape.

"Did that turn out the way you thought it would?"

The Deslonder faced him, looking him in the eye. "What do you think?" he asked. "Are we here? Is Odilon on his ship?"

"Well, er, yes," said Quinn, "but –"

"There you go then," said Zain, serenely surveying the ocean.

Quinn couldn't think of a response, so silence reigned.

"Besides," the Deslonder said suddenly, "it certainly brought you new respect from the others."

Respect was one word for it, Quinn thought. The crew, and even Ash and Ajax to a degree, treated him with a lot more caution than they had previously. He knew they thought his language feat was freakish, but they also knew that Zain held it in great esteem. So far, they'd said nothing to him about it, but Quinn had noticed that Dilly didn't stop to joke around with him like he once had, and Cook actively avoided him.

"People will always fear what they don't understand," said Zain, appearing to read Quinn's mind. "The trick is to show them that what makes you different is nothing to fear."

Quinn nodded. He wasn't sure how to do that. He figured that until he'd worked it out, it was probably best to keep a low profile, so he'd thrown himself into his work.

Now, as he saw Ash and Ajax stop talking and laughing as he came near, and then move over slightly to make room for him, he wondered what the chances were that they might simply forget what they'd seen. Ajax hadn't said much – he seemed to see just how much Quinn *didn't* want to talk about it and seemed happy enough to let it lie for now, though there were questions in his eyes.

But Ash, Quinn knew, was hurt. He'd taken great pains, as his family had always schooled him, to hide his memory from her over the years, and she took it very personally that, as his best friend, she hadn't been trusted with the information. When he'd gently tried to explain that his parents were trying to protect him – look at what had happened to her mother – she'd closed up completely and walked away from him. It had taken a few days for her to unfreeze and talk to him again – and he still had no clear idea what it was he'd said to make her so unhappy. Girls. Who knew what went on in their heads?

Now he sat with them, half listening to what they were talking about – Ash's plants, Ajax's ever-present hunger – and half drifting away with his own thoughts. It was enough just to be near them. Anyone watching them would think he was just a normal boy, talking and laughing with friends. Maybe if he sat here long enough, it would be true.

~

The storm had them in its teeth and was shaking them like a rabid dog. Wave after wave crashed over the deck, the wind howled around them, and the rain came down in thick sheets. Zain was lashed to the tiller, desperately using all his mighty strength to keep them upright and attempt to hold a course. All the portholes and doors were battened, and the sails were tightly furled. Still, Quinn felt as though they were fighting a losing battle. How could a tiny ship like theirs stay atop this boiling cauldron?

Zain had told the three of them to get into the wheelhouse and stay out of the way. It was probably safest, but it was also extremely frustrating. Feeling as though you were being brought to your doom without actually being able to do anything about it didn't make for a comfortable ride.

"Land! Land ho!" screamed Ison, the watch, from the bow. "Port side, bearing fast."

From his position in the wheelhouse, Quinn could see Zain's jaw clench. They'd seen nothing but rocks all the way up this coastline and now the storm was driving the ship towards them!

"What can you see?" Zain shouted hoarsely to Ison, who had lashed his lanky body to the handrail of the ship, and was peering into the rain and sea spray. Zain had deemed it safer to keep the watch off the mast in the terrible conditions.

"Nothing," Ison replied, panic cracking his voice. "Water."

Quinn thought fast. They needed a better view. And now. Somebody needed to go up that mast and with all hands on deck, struggling to keep the sails in position, it was down to him, Ash or Ajax. Unfortunately, they'd discovered during the week that Ajax, so cheerful and unflappable under all circumstances, had just one weakness – he hated heights. He'd gotten about three lengths up the mast before getting dizzy and sliding back down again.

And there was no way he'd sit here while Ash went out into the maelstrom.

"I'll go up as far as I can and see what I can see," Quinn shouted to Zain, reluctantly, hoping the captain would tell him he was being ridiculous.

Zain didn't even look at him, only nodded. Ajax, huddled next to him, grabbed his arm.

"You can't go up there – you'll be blown off!" he shouted.

Quinn stared at him. "Do you want to do it?" he asked, knowing the answer.

Ajax shook his head emphatically.

"Well, then," said Quinn. "Zain needs something to steer towards and we're wasting time!"

With that, he was out the door, and sopping wet in seconds. "Me and my big ideas," he muttered, as he doubled over against the wind, crab-walking towards the forward mast. He began to shimmy slowly up the slippery wood, knowing that every foot gained put him in an ever-precarious position. One strong gust and he'd be blown overboard.

Squinting against the rain, trying to see through the hair now plastered to his forehead, he clutched the mast and scanned the port side of the ship, looking for any lightening of color that might suggest a gap in the coastline – a safe harbor.

Nothing.

He could see broiling white foam, suggesting waves dashing over unseen rocks, bubbling closer and closer. They needed to go forward, and soon, or they would be dashed against those rocks – and survival would not be an option.

Movement behind the boat caught his eye. A shape rising, the water gushing outward in a circle around it. He drew a sharp breath. He'd seen that strange water movement before.

Gripping the pole more tightly, he watched in awe as the Great White Beast rose again from the depths, a pale, glistening outline in the storm. He tried to cry out, but the words wouldn't form. Surely someone else had seen it?

He looked down, desperately searching for Zain, but the captain had eyes only for the rocks looming ever closer.

Quinn's eyes were drawn back to the beast. It came farther out of the water than before, closer to the *Libertas*. In other circumstances, Quinn would be worried it was going to capsize them, but now, with all seeming lost anyway, he could only watch in wonder.

It shot up towards the sky and crashed back into the water. As it did so, the beast started its own procession of waves, which rocked the boat, pushing it along at great speed, propelling it forward. Zain gripped the tiller as the ship passed the rocks and continued out into wide, open space.

Quinn was still watching the space where the beast had been. It did not resurface.

But below him, the watch at the bow started shouting, pointing wildly to the port side. "Cove! Cove!" he shouted. "Cove!"

Zain swung the tiller until the *Libertas* had turned all to port, with the wind and waves now at her stern, pushing her down the channel between two hulking rocky outcrops and into the quieter waters of the tiny harbor beyond. Within minutes, they'd dropped anchor and headed below decks to celebrate and ride out the rest of the storm in relative calm.

They were safe. Beaten, battered, saturated, but safe.

As Quinn slid quietly down the sodden mast to follow everyone else, he began to wonder if he'd imagined the Great White Beast. Was it a fish? A benign spirit? Something from another world? Had it really pushed them to safety?

He shook his head, suddenly realizing how cold and tired he was.

"What's up, Quinn?" asked Ajax, thumping him on the back when he saw him. "Seen a ghost?"

"Maybe," he answered, taking a cup of hot tea from Ash. "Maybe."

They both looked at him expectantly, but he only shook his head. He was going to keep his thoughts about the beast to himself for the time being.

After all, who knew if they'd ever see it again?

Chapter Ten

Quinn was sick of being cold. He was wearing every item of clothing he owned, all at once, and still the icy fingers crept in to chill his skin. The coastline was covered in snow, the water was full of chunks of ice, and, frankly, Quinn had had enough.

By his estimation, they were going to run out of north if they kept going. He was beginning to wonder at the size of this land they'd discovered. It was already more than four times the size of Verdania and showed no signs of abating. Perhaps it was actually a wall that marked the end of the world? He was really struggling to get his head around it. Nothing Master Blau had taught him had prepared him for this.

He could only be thankful that the small cove they'd pulled into for safety during the storm had proved useful for stocking up on their supplies. Their rain barrels were, of course, full of fresh water, but they'd been running perilously low on other supplies. They'd stayed in the cove for two full days and Jericho and Dilly had used the time to go hunting with a bow and the spear they'd liberated from the tribal village. They'd been eating fresh meat courtesy of a large deer the pair had killed, and Ash had been using blocks of ice from the abundant supply around them to keep the extra frozen for later. Their grain stocks were low, but Cook had been stretching them by making broth.

So they weren't going to starve. Not yet. And maybe not before they ran out of ocean on which to sail.

Ajax, of course, was unperturbed. It was now ten days since Odilon had sailed off without him and he seemed quite happy to forget his mapmaker role, and take on a new one as crew member with Zain. He was a hard worker and the crew was more than happy to have him around.

Quinn was beginning to wonder what would happen if they did run into Odilon again. The nobleman was bound to want Ajax back on board the *Fair Maiden* – after all, there was the race to win – but would Ajax want to go?

"What are you doing?" Ash crept up beside him and tucked herself in at his side, for extra warmth.

"Just standing here, quietly freezing," he answered. She laughed. He liked her laugh. It wasn't a girlish giggle like Merryn, his brother Simon's love interest, but a hearty chuckle. She'd managed to keep up the facade of being a boy for months now – he wasn't even sure that Ajax had caught on – but it must have been getting hard for her. He wondered why Zain hadn't told the crew after she'd helped rescue them all in the tent village. Surely there wouldn't have been a better time to show that she wasn't bad luck?

But the captain always had his reasons, so Quinn hadn't brought it up.

"Sail! Ship ahoy!"

Jericho, the day's watch, sounded thrilled to have something to report other than "ice," "ice," "ice."

"Colors?" shouted Zain.

There was a pause as Jericho tried to make out the symbol on the small flag flying, as it did on every ship, from the pole on the stern. "Red, white, blue – yellow X."

Dolan! And Dolan meant Ira. Quinn sighed.

"He's signaling," shouted Jericho. Quinn ran to the other side of the ship so he could see the message, conveyed via the raising and lowering of different flags. It was a simple system, mostly used by sailors to communicate trouble or problems.

Three black flags.

Dolan was in trouble!

"Visible signs of distress?" Zain called to the watch.

"None."

Strange. The ship seemed to be sailing normally enough, no listing to suggest she was taking on water. No smoke to suggest fire.

"Illness?" Quinn asked Zain, sidling over to hear what the captain had to say.

Zain looked thoughtful. "Perhaps? But we'd be crazy to go over there if that's the case."

Good point.

"What then?"

Zain thought a moment. He'd changed direction so that they were sailing directly towards the *Wandering Spirit*, but now, with a deft flick of his fingers, he shifted their course. "Signal 'follow me,'" he told Ison and Abel, who was standing by to signal back.

"It's up to them now," said Zain. "We'll find a safe place to anchor and then see what this is all about."

~

Creepy. It was the only word to describe the bay in which the *Libertas* now sheltered, awaiting the arrival of the *Wandering Spirit*. The shallow inlet was a desolate place, with nothing but snow as far as the eye could see. And yet . . .

To one end lay a stone castle, one that showed many signs of repair, and still sections of wall were crumbling in the icy conditions. Dark and ominous, it loomed against the gray sky.

Who had built it here in this forlorn and forbidding place? Where were they now?

Actually, thought Quinn, wrapping his cloak tighter around him, that probably wasn't a question. The cold would be enough to keep anyone tucked up indoors. No, the real question was the first one. Why build here in the first place?

A long jetty, also showing signs of wear, thrust out into the ocean. Zain sent Jericho out to walk its length before declaring it sound enough to tie the *Libertas* to its creaking pylons. It was an elaborate structure, more suited to a bustling town than an isolated castle, and merely added to the mystery of the place.

Even if it weren't for the fact that a meeting with Ira was mere minutes away (good enough reason to stay on board), Quinn wasn't keen to get off the *Libertas* and explore the unwelcoming cove.

Ajax and Ash were first down the gangplank, and Quinn trailed behind, his enthusiasm waning even further when he saw the huge holes in the jetty, the icy cold green water sucking and calling beneath them. The poles supporting the structure might be sound, but the same couldn't be said for the planking on top.

They continued at a subdued pace, testing each plank before putting their full weight on it. Ajax had the worst time of it – planks that had easily borne the lighter weights of Quinn and Ash creaked ominously under his bulk.

"Zain's going to have a few problems with this," he said, face tight with concentration.

"He's got his hands full with Dolan," said Ash, indicating the two ships behind them. "He probably won't even come ashore."

"We could do with more provisions," said Ajax.

"Always thinking about food," Ash said.

"I'm a growing boy," he said. They all laughed. Ajax's appetite was legendary and Cook constantly grumbled that, between them, he and Zain ate as much as the rest of the crew put together.

"Not too much that's appetizing here," said Quinn, as they finally reached the end of the jetty and stood outside the daunting castle walls.

There was not so much as a bird to be seen. Snow covered the castle forecourt in a blanket and the enormous wooden door to the keep had frozen and cracked.

"How did this happen?" Ajax asked in wonder, touching the splintered door with a gloved hand.

"Water," said Quinn. "The door got wet, the ice grew inside it, and shattered it, same as the jetty."

They were both looking at him. "How do you know that?" Ajax asked.

"Um . . . my father told me," he said, not wanting to admit that he'd read it somewhere, once.

"Oh well, makes it easier to get in," said Ajax, while Ash eyed him suspiciously. "Come on!"

Inside, the dark, gloomy, narrow hall led straight down the center of the building, with rooms off either side.

Narrow slots located high in outer corners of the rooms let in thin stripes of weak sunshine, and Quinn could see his breath on the air.

"It's colder in here than it is out there," he said. It was true. The blue-gray stones seemed to capture the cold and hold it in the hall.

"Over here!" Ash called. She'd run ahead and stood poised in a wide arched opening in the hall – hand to mouth, stiff with horror.

Quinn soon saw why. She was standing in the entrance of what had once been a Great Hall. Slumped over the tables, crisp with ice, amid shattered glasses and overturned chairs, lay at least twenty bodies – men, women and children. It was clear from the half-eaten remains of food on plates that a feast had been interrupted.

The three friends were silent.

"Whoa," said Ajax, finally. "Guess we can see why it's so quiet around here."

"It looks as though it happened only minutes ago," Quinn whispered. Whoever had done this hadn't even stopped to remove the swords from the backs of the three bodies lying across the top table.

"The ice has preserved them, like it does our venison," said Ash, in hushed tones.

Quinn shuddered. The comparison between these people and meat was a bit close for his liking.

"We need to tell Zain," he said. "I'm not sure who did this, but if there's any chance they're still here . . ."

They turned as one and thundered out of the hall as though the dead would rise up and follow them.

~

Ira had not changed. He stood on the deck of the *Libertas*, feet wide apart, looking down his nose at everyone and everything on board.

"So you can see why you must give us provisions," Dolan was telling Zain. Quinn and the others had arrived back at the *Libertas*, out of breath and full of their story, only to find a full parley was in session – an official meeting of two sides to discuss important issues. There was no choice but to sit, bursting with information of what they'd seen, and wait until the parley was over.

Ira looked at them as though they were rabble, though his brow furrowed as he caught sight of Ajax, and he shifted closer to Dolan, as though to reinforce his position at the explorer's right hand.

Zain attempted a polite smile, though once again Quinn would have called it more a baring of teeth. Cleric Greenfield, who had been called out by Dolan as the "supervisor" of their expedition, shook his head bemused.

The cleric had worked his way into the hearts of everyone on board the *Libertas*. He was a kindly old man, happy enough to keep to himself unless sought out, and keep them afloat with his prayers. He did not interfere with Zain's captaincy, and Zain took great care to always keep him abreast of the ship's daily progress. He knew that the King had chosen Cleric Greenfield precisely because he would not keep too close an eye on proceedings, but that didn't mean that respect wasn't due.

Dolan, however, did not know this. With the disdainful attitude of one who was not born to nobility but who believed he had earned the right to be treated as better than most, he would not speak to Zain, whom he saw as a mere slave. The Deslonder's inclusion in the race was still, after many months, a thorn in his side and a great topic of derisive conversation aboard the *Wandering Spirit*.

He truly believed that he was entitled to half the provisions on board the *Libertas*. If a slave had them, then he should have them.

The cleric was not, however, convinced. "So, you are telling me," he said in his ponderous way, "that you have not managed to restock your own supplies, so we should give you half of ours. To keep the race fair?"

"Precisely," said Dolan, clapping his hands together once, as though rewarding a star pupil. "So if you'll just give half of everything you have, we'll be on our way."

The cleric held up his hand.

"But you have not explained why you have allowed your position to become so precarious," he said.

Ira rolled his eyes. Dolan was too adult to do anything that obvious, but Quinn could hear the eye roll in his voice.

"Why, it has been a long and difficult journey," he said.

"Yes," said Cleric Greenfield. "For all of us."

Quinn hid a smile. He was elderly, this man, but he was no fool. His mild manner belied a sharp mind, as Quinn had discovered during many conversations over a game of chip and dice. The cleric could talk knowledgeably about many subjects – and slay an opponent at the same time.

Dolan could see that he was not going to get away with pat explanations.

"We, er, ran into some bad luck – a monster, in fact! It was huge, with gnashing teeth and fiery eyes. We had to fight long and hard to get past it. But in the end we were triumphant."

Quinn and Zain exchanged glances. They were both remembering the day that they had seen the *Wandering Spirit* change course suddenly. The day of the Great White Beast. Or Day One of the Great White Beast, Quinn amended, remembering the most recent storm.

"I see," said Cleric Greenfield, who had his own hazy memories of the Great White Beast. "But this doesn't explain the provision situation."

Dolan shifted his feet. "We, er, had to change direction suddenly during the fight and ended up much farther north than we'd expected. Fresh supplies have not been easy to come by. We prayed for assistance but –"

He stopped short, as though struck by inspiration.

"We prayed for assistance and your sail appeared on the horizon!" he finished triumphantly.

Quinn heard Zain mutter under his breath.

The cleric nodded. An intervention from his god was the one thing he could not argue against. "Well, if that's the case, I see no reason not to equip you with some provisions," he said.

Angry chatter broke out amongst the *Libertas* crew, while Ira and Dolan smiled smugly.

"However," said the cleric, holding up his hand, "I see no reason that you would need half. Zain has provided well for our crew. It seems that you have been set a challenge to do the same for yours."

Quinn hid a smile at Dolan's angry expression. Food of any kind would be hard to come by in the desolate wastelands around which they now sailed. Quinn knew Zain had been eking out their own provisions to make them last as long as possible, not knowing when the next chance would come to stock up. Supplies were one of the biggest challenges for long-distance explorers. Zain had told Quinn that he had chosen the *Libertas*, the plainest ship available, precisely because she was well and simply made, making repairs on the run easier, and because she had, for her size, the largest cargo space of any ship in the fleet.

Zain had also used the promissory note, 1,000 deckerts, a small fortune, given to each explorer by the King as a ship's fund, to stock the *Libertas* to the gunnels with dried beans, sea biscuits, flour and salted meats. Dolan and Odilon, Quinn knew, had both taken on board sweetmeats and wine, intended to keep them more comfortable. Zain ate the same as his crew – plain and simple – and Quinn knew that meant they would all eat longer. The leftover deckerts Zain had converted to gold ingots, knowing that these would be more useful anywhere they ended up.

Even so, you couldn't eat gold.

"Very well, then," said Dolan. "We will take what you can spare."

He made it sound as though *he* were doing *them* a favor, thought Quinn. Given the way Ajax snorted, he hadn't missed the inference either.

Cook was called and the haggling began. In the end, Dolan and Ira left the ship with one sack of salted flour, a portion of venison and two different kinds of dried beans. Survival rations. Quinn had not missed the way in which Dolan's eyes had widened at the sight of the venison, and he was not surprised when Zain ordered a watch on the ship when they later went ashore.

~

"Stabbed in the back, you say?" asked Zain, stroking his chin thoughtfully. He, Quinn, Ajax and Ash were all sitting cross-legged on the deck. Quinn had thought he might burst with the news of all they'd seen at the castle, but first he'd had to wait until Dolan and Ira were back on the *Wandering Spirit* and then for Zain to organize Jericho, Cleaver, Dilly and Ison into a hunting party. But Zain would not be diverted from his task. Dolan might be happy to subsist on handouts, but Zain knew they were sailing into even harder territory. If there was food to be had in this godforsaken place, Zain's crew would find it. "What race were they?" he asked now.

Ajax, Ash and Quinn looked at each other. The truth was, they'd been so startled by the sight of the dead men in that eerie place that they hadn't looked that closely.

"Er, they were blue," said Ash. The others nodded.

Zain grimaced. "That would be the cold," he said. "They're frozen. What about under that?"

"There was a layer of ice," said Quinn. "It was hard to tell."

"So you can't tell me anything except that they were all dead and there were swords?"

"It was kind of hard to look past that," said Quinn, defensively.

Zain stood. "Okay, show me."

Leaving Abel on watch, sword in hand, and Cleric Greenfield in his cabin below, the party set off carefully along the jetty. They had to move in single file, with large gaps between them, to ensure their weight was as evenly distributed as possible. Eventually, though, they were all in the castle forecourt.

Ajax led the way back into the castle keep, and they were soon back in the Great Hall. They felt braver with Zain beside them, and so took the time to look around more closely.

Now they could see that the slain people were fair-haired and, under the blue, fair skinned. "They're Northerners," said Zain, surprised, adding quietly, "what are they doing here?"

As King Orel's personal slave, he'd been privy to many of the secrets of State. Nobody noticed a silent slave when they were discussing important matters – particularly one who was always by the King's side. But he'd never heard anyone speak of exploration by the Northerners, who were farmers and fishermen, let alone settlement. And it was a difficult thing to keep quiet.

"And what happened to them?" asked Quinn. He gestured expansively, taking in the mess around them.

"This is no place for us," Zain said, decisively. "We cannot help them and we want no part of what happened here. We will get the others and go."

The sudden move took the others by surprise. But they didn't hesitate to follow him as he strode towards the entrance.

It was only as they approached the keep's main entrance

that the shouting and clanging of swords began to filter through from outside.

Zain broke into a run, with the others hard at his heels.

By the time they reached the shore, however, it was all over. Dolan and Ira were vaulting up the gangplank of the *Wandering Spirit*, as their crew set sail. On the *Libertas*, all was quiet. Too quiet.

Worse than that, however, was the large section of jetty, between their ship and the shore, that was now missing.

Chapter Eleven

Quinn's blood ran as cold as the air around him. They were stranded on an icy beach, the scene of a massacre, with no way to get back to their ship. And Dolan and Ira were sailing gaily towards the bay entrance, waving from the stern of the *Wandering Spirit.*

Zain put his fingers in his mouth and whistled, three ear-piercing short bursts. Moments later, Jericho appeared at the other end of the cove. Dilly, Cook, Ison and Cleaver also materialized out of the frozen landscape, running to their captain.

"What's going on?" shouted Jericho.

"Dolan," said Zain, and the word came out like a curse. "My bet is that he's stolen the rest of our supplies. Or as much as he could get his hands on."

How much could that be? Quinn thought. Surely they hadn't been within the castle walls for that long?

"We need to get out there and find out," Zain continued. "The question is how?"

Jericho and the crew looked askance at the broken section of jetty. "Ash is a good swimmer," said Jericho. Ash paled at the thought of walking into the icy water.

"Nobody's swimming today," said Zain. "They'd freeze to death before they were wet."

"What then?" asked Jericho.

"Quinn and Ash," said Zain. "You two are the lightest – go out on the jetty as far as you can and see if you can get an idea of exactly how wide that gap is."

They nodded, and immediately began picking their way out towards the ship. "Be careful, Ash," said Quinn. "That missing section may have weakened the rest of the structure." And, indeed, the whole jetty seemed to wobble more vigorously under them as they tiptoed out.

When they were as close as they dared to go to the end, Quinn could see that the jetty's collapse was not complete – the missing section had been broken, but had not disappeared beneath the waves. The supporting poles were still in place. But there was no way to get from where they were to the other side.

"How wide do you think that is?" asked Ash.

Quinn calculated rapidly. "About twenty paces."

"Not that far, then."

"Far enough," he answered.

His mind whirled, searching for a solution. Even if there was something on the ship they could use to bridge the gap, they had no way of getting to it. The ominous silence on board continued. Surely if Abel and the Cleric were able to move they would have done so by now?

"Come on," he said. "Let's go tell the others."

By the time they returned to where the others waited, Quinn had racked his brain but to no avail. He quickly outlined the situation.

"Twenty paces might as well be one hundred," said Jericho, disconsolately. "We're stuck!"

Zain would not give up so easily. "Scour the area for anything we can use to cross that gap," he said.

Ten minutes later, they were all back on the beach. The stark landscape had given up its bounty: three small pieces of driftwood.

"That's not enough to even burn," said Jericho. "We're doomed!"

"Will you shut up?" said Zain, firmly. "What about the castle – anything there?"

"Mostly stone," said Ajax. "No use."

"What about the doors?" said Quinn. "That big door to the keep?"

"It's too small," said Ash. "It's huge for a door, but it's not twenty paces."

"Yes, but it's splitting," said Quinn. "What if we could get two pieces of it and somehow fix them together?"

They ran as one to the keep door, and began pulling at the split shards, which continued to break in their hands.

"It's no use," puffed Ajax. "We can't get big enough pieces."

"Aaaargh!" Zain roared as another piece of wood splintered. His growing frustration was apparent, and it was this fracturing of the Deslonder's usual unbreachable calm that brought home to Quinn the seriousness of the situation. His mind raced through images of the castle's interior, seeking out anything that could help them.

"Ah!" said Quinn, slapping himself on the forehead. "How could I be so stupid? The tables!"

"Tables?" said Jericho.

"Tables!" echoed Zain, racing off down the hallway. "Of course. Ajax! With me!"

Within minutes, they were back, carrying a long feasting table between them. Putting it down, they went back inside. From memory, Quinn knew there were three: the shorter top table, and two longer ones.

Would they be long enough? Quickly, as the crew watched, he paced out the table's length. Eight paces. Zain and Ajax returned with the next table. Six paces. They would have twenty-two paces of table to work with.

Quinn hoped it would be enough.

"Now we need to find a way to fix them together," he said, as Zain and Ajax returned with the last table. "And to get the legs off."

"That bit's easy," said Ajax, leaning his full weight against the wood. The table legs buckled and snapped. He proceeded to work on the next set.

Quinn realized that everyone else was looking at him. He needed a solution to fix the tables together into a bridge

"We have no nails," Quinn said, thinking aloud. "But we do have an abundance of wood splinters . . ."

"Yes . . . and . . ." said Zain, prompting him. Quinn could see hope in the faces of all the men around him.

"But they're very fragile, as we've seen," he said, "I'm not sure they'd hold our weight."

"They don't need to hold all our weight," said Ash. "Just enough for one person to get across and bring the longboat back for the others."

"The longboat is too much for one person," said Zain.

"Okay, two then," said Ash. "As you said, Quinn and I are the lightest. We'll go."

Quinn laughed impatiently. "Go where?" he asked. "We haven't even solved the first problem yet."

"Yes, but you will," she said. "And when you do I'll be ready."

Quinn wished he were as confident as she was. But what was the alternative? No one else was stepping forward with a plan. He thought about his father and Jed, fixing the barn, mending fences. He might be better with a needle than a mallet, but he had *seen* it done.

"Okay, then," he said. "Who's got a knife?"

Everyone raised a hand. Except him. Once again he cursed his lack of weaponry. "We need to whittle some nails," he said, demonstrating with his hands. "Broader at the top, this long and with a very sharp point," he said.

"How many?" asked Ajax.

Quinn thought. "Eighteen," he said. If he and Ash had to walk across a bridge held together with a few splinters of questionable wood, the least he could do was to make it as solid as possible. He'd use three nails on top of each tabletop, and three underneath. The worst part was that he'd need to allow minimum overlap for each sheet of wood, which meant that the joins would be weak.

Best not to think about it now.

~

It took two men on each side to maneuver the "bridge" along the jetty, moving as carefully as they could under its weight. As they began to slide it over the water towards the other side, Quinn could only hope that a) it was long enough and b) it was strong enough to make the journey without breaking at the middle join. He realized he was holding his breath.

"Just makes it," shouted Zain from his position at the very end of their side of the jetty. The four men made their way back to the beach where Quinn and Ash were standing.

"Okay," said Zain. "Your turn."

Quinn saw Ash's hand move towards his in an instinctive bid for security. Fortunately, at the last minute she remembered she was supposed to be a boy and snatched it back to her side.

"Ready?" he asked her.

"Ready," she said, looking anything but. They both knew that if the bridge collapsed under them, they would drown in the freezing water in seconds. They walked out to the start of the bridge. Beneath it, the green water bubbled and boiled, swirling around the remaining structure poles (which were just too wide to help support the tabletop bridge).

"I'll go first," said Quinn, firmly. It was his idea. If it failed, it should be he who paid the price.

She nodded.

He put his foot on the tabletop, testing it with his weight. It shifted under him, bowing at the joints, but seemed stable enough.

"Go quickly, on the balls of your feet," said Ash. "Like the barn rafters at home. The more time you spend on it, the heavier you get."

It was his turn to nod. Then, taking a deep breath, he charged across the bridge, feeling it spring and swing under him. Towards the end, he took a flying leap, landing with a crash on the old jetty, which groaned in protest.

Ash clapped her hands. "Well done!" she said, before following him across as lightly as a sprite in the forest.

Once she was beside him, they both ran as fast as they could to where the *Libertas* was, creaking on her mooring.

"Abel!" called Quinn through cupped hands as they approached, hoping desperately for an answer.

And there it was, faint, and coming from the bowels of the ship, but there.

"They're alive!" said Quinn, crashing up the gangplank and leaping onto the deck. "Come on, Ash! They're alive!"

But when they got below deck, they found only Cleric Greenfield, locked in his cabin.

"What happened?" asked Quinn, as they opened the door. "Where's Abel?"

"I don't know," said the cleric, indignantly. "Dolan came back and asked to see me in my cabin, for some guidance. He followed me down here, and then locked me in before I knew what was happening."

Quinn and Ash exchanged glances. "You wait here," said Ash. "We'll have a look around."

The cleric nodded gratefully.

Back on deck, Quinn and Ash searched every inch for the missing crewman. There was no sign.

"At least there's no blood," said Quinn.

"Yeah," said Ash, balefully. "At least they stopped short of killing their own countryman. Unless they've stuffed his body below deck. Or thrown it overboard."

There was no answer to that. They continued their search through the cabins below and finally down into the hull. The storeroom door was wide-open, confirming Zain's fear that it had been supplies that Dolan was after. Inside, they found Abel, flat on the floor, bleeding from the head.

"He figured out what was going on and tried to stop them," guessed Ash, rushing to Abel's side. "He's breathing, but it's shallow. We need to get him upstairs and warmed up."

"We can't carry him," said Quinn. "Wait here!" He ran to his bed, grabbing the thick woolen blanket off the top, as well as a sheet. "Here," he said, thrusting them at Ash. "Put that on him and I thought you might use the sheet for a bandage or something."

She nodded and set to work. Meanwhile, Quinn scanned the storeroom, noting that while it wasn't completely empty, Dolan had stolen more than three-quarters of the stores that had been there.

"The whole crew must have followed them over," he said, angrily. "They've taken nearly everything, including all the venison."

She looked up from wrapping a small piece of sheet around the still-bleeding cut on Abel's head. "But what will we eat?" she said, fearfully. "They've only left a week or two's worth of food here, and that's only if we eat gruel every day."

Given their location, and the fact that the landscape continued to grow harsher, it wasn't likely that they'd be able to do a major restock any time soon either.

"I don't know. All I know is that we need to go and get the others as quickly as we can. Hopefully, Zain will know what to do."

~

Zain didn't know what to do. Quinn could tell as soon as he apprised him of the situation in the longboat on the way back to the *Libertas*. The captain's face was as impassive as ever, but Quinn had seen the flash of fear in his eyes before he'd been able to hide it.

Starvation was every explorer's nightmare, and a reality for every one of them.

Back on board, chaos reigned for a while, while everyone cursed Dolan and the ocean and the frozen landscape around them. Being practical men, it didn't take long before thoughts turned to what to do next. How to solve the problem that faced them.

"Why don't we just keep sailing and hope something turns up?" asked Jericho.

Zain stroked his chin. The normally clean-shaven captain had allowed his beard to grow as they traveled north. Quinn could only envy him the extra warmth afforded by the luxuriant facial hair.

"It may be our only option," he said. "But I believe that food will become scarcer the farther north we go. And it's the lack of flour and beans that will become our biggest problem. Without them, we have no reserves."

Everybody sat silently for a moment, considering the day when the food might run out.

"Is it worth having another look around that castle?" asked Ajax. "We never got farther than the Great Hall."

Zain laughed harshly. "I'm sure any food in there has been carried off by whomever killed those people," he said. "But you are more than welcome to go. And bring back those swords. I want another look at them. It's one thing to kill people – quite another to leave a sword behind."

"I'll go with you," said Quinn. All this sitting around in the cold talking about starvation was making him nervous. And hungry.

"I'll stay and watch Abel," said Ash. She'd made Abel as comfortable as possible in Quinn's bed, deeming his own hammock too unstable for a man with head injuries. Quinn wanted to ask her how she knew this stuff, but didn't want to bring her mam up again after their last conversation.

Cleric Greenfield was down in his cabin, writing a letter to the King explaining Dolan's behavior. Quinn wasn't quite sure how he thought the letter would get to the King, but at least it kept the cleric busy and had stopped him apologizing over and over – which had been getting on everyone's already tightening nerves.

Now, as he and Ajax made the crossing back to the beach in the longboat, shadows lengthening as the sun began to set, Quinn found himself wondering if this very long day could get any stranger.

Once on the beach, they quickly made their way to the Great Hall, where Ajax took on the task of pulling out the swords. Holding the ornate weapons gingerly by the hilts, they returned to the door, and piled them up to take back to the *Libertas* with them.

"Do we split up?" asked Ajax, as they turned back into the castle.

"Do you want to?" asked Quinn. There was a very good chance that the castle was deserted, but even so, it was an eerie and unsettling place.

"It would make sense . . . but not really." The big redhead grinned down at him. "Safety in numbers and all that."

Quinn grinned back. "Yes, two of us will make all the difference," he jested, but he felt better. He hadn't looked forward to entering those dark, cold spaces on his own. With Ajax by his side, it felt more like a game.

"Let's start at the top," said Ajax.

"Isn't it more likely that any food store would be down below?"

"Probably," grinned Ajax, "but don't you want to have a good look around?"

Not really, thought Quinn, but he smiled back. "Oh right, yeah, of course."

The keep was laid out conventionally, three stories with a solar, the Lord of the castle's working room and retreat, at the top. The furniture was still there, beds, tables and chairs made from rough-hewn wood. Quinn couldn't think where it might have come from, nor the stone for that matter, given the desolate landscape around them.

When they got to the door of the solar, they stopped.

"There's been a fight in here," said Ajax, looking at the mess in front of them.

Quinn shook his head slowly, taking in the overturned tables, and the drawers and boxes open on the floor. "Not a fight," he said. "A search. Someone was looking for something. Something they wanted badly."

"I wonder what it could be," said Ajax.

Quinn picked his way over the debris on the floor. "I wonder if they found it," he said.

"Should we look for it?"

Quinn laughed. "What would we be looking for?"

"It must be something really valuable," said Ajax. "Why else would someone go to so much trouble? The least we could do is have a quick scout around. You know, given that there's a treasure component to the race and all . . ."

"Yes," agreed Quinn. "But there is the small point that we're meant to be looking for food. Without food it won't matter about treasure. We won't even finish the race."

"Aw, come on," said Ajax. "If there's food here, five minutes won't make any difference. I don't reckon anyone's been alive here for weeks."

Quinn sighed. Ajax was right. They were on a fool's mission as it was.

"Okay, you take that side and I'll take this side." They began poking through the boxes and drawers on the floor. A few minutes later, Ajax stopped.

"This is useless," he said. "If the treasure was here, they'd have definitely found it." He stood up, scanning the walls.

"We don't know that they didn't," reminded Quinn, "because we don't even know what we're looking for."

But Ajax didn't move. "What if it was really well hidden and they didn't have time to look properly?"

"What do you mean?" asked Quinn, coming to stand beside him.

"Well, if I was going to hide something in here, it wouldn't be in a drawer or something that was in the open, now, would it?"

"No," said Quinn, slowly.

"Cleric Fennelly has a secret stone in his parlor," said Ajax. "It turns and there's a space behind it."

"You think there might be one here?" Quinn was skeptical. They'd gone from arriving in the solar to searching for possible treasure to secret stones in the blink of an eye. But then he remembered his thoughts about this being more like a game with Ajax, and decided he might as well continue to play along for at least a few more minutes.

"Let's find out," Ajax said. "You take that side of the room. Look for a stone that's slightly different. Not enough to be obvious. The mortar will be looser or lighter."

Shaking his head, Quinn, nonetheless, did as he was told. Nothing. He moved to the wall and began tapping them, more for something to do than because he thought anything would come of it.

Tap. Tap. Tap. Thud.

He poked at the stone again. It sounded different from the others.

"Ajax! I think there's something here."

He began prodding around the stone, trying to feel for looseness. Ajax was at his side in seconds, and he began trying to pry the stone loose.

Nothing.

"Maybe I imagined it," said Quinn.

"It doesn't look any different from the others," Ajax said, eyes roving over the wall.

"But there's definitely a different sound . . ." Quinn insisted, tapping at the stone, before trying to pry it again. Nothing.

"Open up!" Quinn said, hammering at the stone three times in frustration. To his surprise, a small section of the wall to his right and up above his head suddenly swung open.

"You did it!" said Ajax. "That one must be a trigger stone for the real secret stone. Ingenious!"

Quinn had to agree. The stone under his hands had turned and, peering inside, he could see that it was connected to the other section with a length of chain. As he'd pushed one side of his stone, the chain had tightened, opening the secret stone.

"What's in there?" he asked Ajax, who was reaching up above his head and feeling around.

"Nothing," Ajax said, looking disappointed. "Nothing at all. The other searchers must have found it."

"Get a chair and have a proper look," said Quinn. "Maybe you're not reaching all the way back."

Ajax pulled a chair over and hoisted himself up on it. "You're right," he said. "It goes a lot farther back than you'd think."

He reached his arm in, right up to the shoulder. "I hope spiders can't live in the cold," he said. "I hate spiders." Quinn smiled – a smile that broadened to earsplitting when he saw Ajax's hand emerge into the light, clasping a tapestry tube, tied with a ribbon.

"What is it?" he asked.

Ajax jumped down from the chair, placing the tapestry on the floor and unrolling it.

"Just a rug," he said, his disappointment back. "Why would you go to all that trouble for a rug?"

Quinn stared down at the tapestry, trying to make sense of it. It was well made, with tight stitches and intricate colors. Black lines were woven throughout the greens, blues and golds, with black dots scattered randomly throughout. He put his face closer, hoping to make sense of the pattern. Nothing.

Quinn pulled back. "Wait a minute!" he shouted. He jumped up onto the chair on which Ajax had stood to put more distance between himself and the rug. "Leif's boots!"

"Leif's boots, what?" said Ajax. "It will look great on your mam's wall?"

Quinn laughed. "Not quite. But it will look great on the wheelhouse wall. It's a map, Ajax! It's a map of the whole area. That large black dot is the castle, and it shows the coastline as far north as it goes and then east."

Ajax looked up at him, eyes shining. "So half our work is done for us?"

Quinn sobered. "Well, yes," he said. "Assuming we don't need to eat it to survive."

They rolled the rug up quickly and hurried down the dark, internal staircase.

"Quinn?" Ajax was leaping down the stairs two at a time. "Can I ask you one question?"

Quinn didn't waste his breath responding, simply nodding.

"Who in heaven's name is Leif – and what do his boots have to do with anything?"

Quinn laughed out loud, stopping three steps from the bottom. "I have *no* idea," he said. "It's just something my father says. We all say it."

Thoughts of his family at home crowded into his head, but he pushed them away. There was no time for reminiscing now.

Ajax scratched his head. "I thought his boots must be really important."

"They are," said Quinn, with a chuckle. "They allow you to curse without upsetting your mam. There is no more important purpose for any footwear anywhere in the world. Now come on!" With that, he leapt the last few steps, landing lightly on his feet, and raced off, Ajax close behind.

A hurried examination of the floors below the Great Hall turned up nothing but a dungeon, empty of all signs of life, and another door that led to the cesspit, where all the castle's waste had been dumped. They backed out of that room at great speed.

"Where's the kitchen?" asked Ajax.

Quinn slapped himself on the forehead – realizing it was becoming quite a habit. "There must be a smaller building out back. It will be there. I guess even in the cold they had to be careful of the fire hazard."

Leaving the keep through the front door, for what Quinn hoped was the last time, they clattered around the courtyard to see what was behind. Sure enough, a small stone building sat just feet from the back of the castle.

"There's no door," said Ajax. "How did they get the food inside?"

"Tunnel, maybe?" said Quinn. "It wouldn't stay hot for long if you had to take it out into the cold."

Sighing, they made their way into the castle. In a small room along the back wall, they found the entrance to a tunnel.

Inside the kitchen, the remains of the last meal lay scattered about. The larder door stood open, and every shelf had been cleared by the raiding party, for that was what Quinn now thought had happened here. The Northerners had come to this isolated place, for whatever reason, and had established a stronghold here. But not strong enough. A raiding party had arrived – under guise of friendship, he thought, for why else would they have been let in the great castle gate – and had attacked from within, taking anything of value with them.

The question was, had they come for the map, or had their search in the solar been coincidental?

"Down here," said Ajax, pulling up a trapdoor in the floor of the larder. "This would be where they kept their stores."

He disappeared down the ladder, and Quinn followed, not very hopefully. It wasn't like the raiders would have missed this trapdoor.

And yet, when they got into the large cellar, they discovered sacks of grain. The wine shelves had been emptied. But the grain remained. The question was why.

"Maybe it's rancid?" suggested Ajax.

"Only one way to find out," said Quinn, taking out Ash's kitchen knife and slitting one of the bags. Wheat began spilling from the sack.

"It looks all right," he said. "I think the cold has preserved it. It's almost frozen."

"Then why did they leave it?" asked Ajax.

"They didn't need it," said Quinn. "Their hold was full of treasure!"

They looked at each other, and began to laugh. The irony was that to them the grain and the map were the greatest treasure they could ever have hoped to find.

~

That night, as the *Libertas* plowed her way north through the rippling ocean, Quinn and Zain rolled the rug out on the wheelhouse floor. "You need to get higher to really see the detail," Quinn explained. "But it shows the coast continuing north and then heading west again."

"The borders of this land," said Zain, thoughtfully. "It is good to know what lies ahead."

"I think the best part is that it seems to present an outline of the whole top of the country," said Quinn, pointing to a line that headed west and then began to drop south again. "They'd gotten no farther south, but do you see the wheat sheaf there?"

Zain nodded.

"I think it's their symbol for food," said Quinn, who'd spent time examining the map while the crew hauled sacks of frozen grain from the cellar to the ship. "See, it's here and here, as well."

He pointed to two other spots farther north on the interior of the map. "Here, they've drawn fish," he said. "So I'm assuming we'll have luck with edible fish there."

"They've been in that castle for some time," said Zain. "It's taken many years to pull this map together."

"Clever of them to make a tapestry as well," said Quinn. "Vellum would have been too fragile in the cold."

Zain was quiet. "Those swords are Gelynion," he said.

Quinn's thoughts whirled. He knew that King Orel had been inspired to create the race after learning of a Gelynion world map. Could it have been those explorers who did this?

"Didn't you say that you thought those bodies were only a few weeks old, despite the cold?" asked Quinn.

"I did. Which makes me think that we are not the only ones out here."

Quinn shivered. The Gelynions were known to be a cruel, ruthless race. Looking at what had happened in that castle, he could only hope that their crew wouldn't get any closer to them.

"Do you think they were looking for the map?" he asked.

Zain sat back on his heels, looking down at the tapestry. "I don't know," he said. "But I can only imagine that to be the case."

"Let's hope they don't find out we have it then," said Quinn, fervently.

Chapter Twelve

"Will they survive?"

Ash turned from her plants in the three wooden bowls, clustered on the window ledge in Quinn's cabin. Each morning she took them up on deck, poured a little rainwater on them, and left them to "take the sun," such as it was. A few hours later, she brought them back down, out of the blustery winds.

"I think they need more light," she said, as worried as a mother with a child. "They're not thriving."

Indeed, the plants looked woebegone, with their droopy leaves.

"Why are they so important to you?" Quinn asked her.

"I want to see what they are," she said. "Plants have so much to offer us . . . Besides, that entire village seemed to be living on them. They might come in handy."

"Have to be better than gruel," he said, grimacing. They

weren't hungry, it was true, but having eaten nothing but gruel for weeks on end, he was ready to give anything a try.

"No sign of any fruit, sorry," she said, turning back to the plants. "And I don't think these ones are about the leaves – they just don't smell like something you'd eat."

He'd noticed himself that the plants had an acidic scent – cooped up in his cabin with them, it was hard to miss.

"Oh well, if anyone can keep them alive, you can," he said.

She blushed. "Nothing to report out there?" she asked, changing the subject.

"Not unless you count water, ice and snow. The coast is all white. If it hadn't been for that map, I'd have wondered whether there was ever going to be any end to it by now."

He still found himself wondering how accurate the rug was. Surely there could be no sources of food up here. It felt instead as though they'd just sail on, into this silent world of white, forevermore. Perhaps this was, in fact, the end of the world. You didn't fall off, you just sailed on and on into . . . what?

He sighed. Thinking about this stuff hadn't gotten any easier, even though he was now out here, in the middle of it. His head still hurt.

"I'm going to see what Zain thinks," he told Ash.

She laughed. "About what? He's not exactly the master of conversation."

It was true that Zain had been even quieter than usual lately. Quinn had seen him, late at night, polishing the three Gelynion swords, studying their markings closely. But he hadn't spoken to Quinn any further about them, or about much else.

Each day he was on deck early, guiding the crew through training. Despite the cold, Quinn loved those morning sessions. He was getting the hang of the techniques Zain was showing them – a fact that he'd demonstrated in no uncertain terms that very day when he'd taken Ajax by surprise and flipped him up and over his head – with a resounding crash as he'd landed flat on his back. He'd tried to be sympathetic when Ajax had protested, but could barely contain his secret smile. Zain had seen, and had smiled back approvingly, warming Quinn all over.

"I don't know," he said now to Ash. "He might be feeling chatty."

"Yeah, well, good luck with that," she called out to him as he exited his cabin.

Up on deck, Quinn found Zain at the tiller as usual, eyes fixed on the horizon.

"Have you marked our position?" the Deslonder asked him.

Quinn gulped. He'd gone downstairs to do just that and had been distracted by Ash and her plants. "No," he admitted. "But I will."

"You might want to add that to your drawing," said Zain, pointing to the coast.

Quinn swung around to see what had caught his eye.

"It's a light!" he shouted. "Where's it coming from?" He squinted up at the lookout platform, but it was empty.

Zain shrugged. "I know as much as you do. I think we'll swing in and take a look though. What do you think?"

Quinn ran to the wheelhouse, where the rug had been fixed to the wall. "It's marked as a food source," he told Zain on his return. "What could it be?"

As they drew closer, they could see that what they'd thought was one light was actually a cluster, close together, shining weakly through the misty air.

"Could it be a village?" asked Quinn.

By now, Ash, Ajax and all other available crew members had huddled in the bow of the ship. Even the cleric had ventured up for a look.

"Why would there be a village all the way up here?" asked Ajax. "Who would live there?"

"Why does anyone live anywhere?" retorted Quinn. "Who lived in that castle? What was the name of that tribe we ran from? It's strange to think of all these people out here, going about their lives, and we didn't even know this part of the world existed until we got here."

"The world's been here the whole time," said Zain, coming up behind them. "Just because we hadn't left home to find it didn't mean there was nothing here."

They thought about that. "Did you know we would find something?" asked Quinn.

Zain shook his head. "No," he said. "But look at us. I am Deslonder, you are Verdanian. Why should the world end at our borders?"

"Er, because until we took this journey, it did," said Ajax.

"No," said Zain, shaking his head again. "What we *knew* about the world ended at our borders. There's a difference."

They were silent, watching as the twinkling lights grew closer and closer. As they got nearer to the coastline, the lights disappeared, only to come back, stronger than ever, as they rounded a bend and found themselves at the mouth of a deep, natural harbor.

"It's beautiful," whispered Ash, taking in the sheer cliffs topped in snow and the navy-blue waters of the harbor. A small collection of buildings, positioned at the very center of the shore, gleamed in the sun.

"They're so white," said Quinn. "Almost as though they're –"

"Made of ice," finished Zain. "It's a port made from ice."

Even the pier and its row of moorings looked as though they'd been carved from a glacier, their surfaces smooth and shining in the weak sunlight. Zain went back to the tiller to ease the *Libertas* in alongside the gleaming jetty, and they tied the ship to the available ice posts.

“Is it secure?” asked Quinn.

“Looking at the thickness of that post, she’s not going anywhere,” Zain reassured him. “Let’s go and see if there’s a harbormaster.”

So far, no one had come out to either challenge their presence or to welcome them, but it didn’t feel desolate, like the castle. It felt more as though everyone had gone home for lunch. The town, such as it was, lay at the end of the jetty, on either side of a makeshift road.

“That might be a good place to start,” said Zain, pointing to the largest building, on the left side of the jetty. It was a single-story structure, with a strange, rounded roofline. As they drew closer, Quinn could see that it was constructed entirely from ice bricks, which locked together to form the walls and continued up and over to create the roof. Smoke was rising through a hole in the center.

“That’s the weirdest-looking building I’ve ever seen!” he said.

“Seen a lot of buildings, have you?” asked Zain.

“Oh, you know, one or two.”

“One or two that all looked the same as your house and your neighbor’s?”

“Maybe.”

“The buildings in Deslond have roofs that shape,” said Zain, a faraway look in his eyes. “Not made from ice, but domed and beautiful.”

Quinn filed that away. With any luck they would find Deslond on their travels. If indeed the world was round, they should pass it at some point. He would like to see the buildings that put that look on Zain's weathered face.

As they approached the large building, Quinn was surprised to see that it was locked with a stout, thoroughly conventional wooden door. It had been fitted within a wooden frame and he could see long bolts protruding deep into the ice to keep it secure.

Zain knocked on the door.

Nothing.

"Maybe nobody's home," joked Ajax.

Zain looked around. "And they left a fire burning?"

"Not particularly safety conscious?" tried Ajax.

Zain's response was somewhere between a harrumph and a spit.

Ajax said nothing further.

Zain knocked again, a thud, thud, thud that would be hard to ignore even if you were asleep – or dead.

And finally they heard a fumbling sound as the bolt on the inside was raised.

"H-he-hello?" A pale, scrawny boy with fair hair peered around the door. Quinn noted the boy's use of Suspite.

"Greetings, young master," said Zain, in the same language, causing Quinn's eyebrows to shoot up in surprise. It seemed he wasn't the only one with language secrets. "We are travelers, looking for food and rest."

"Er, there's none here," said the boy, standing up to his full height, which, Quinn figured, made him as tall as Quinn's shoulder. "So you should probably clear off."

The crew muttered behind them. They didn't understand what was being said, but the boy's tone told them everything.

Zain silenced them with a gesture. "Sorry – did you say 'clear off'?" he enquired politely, shaking his head in disbelief. "Is there anyone, er, more senior than you that we could talk to?"

"Just leave us alone," the boy responded stoutly, though Quinn could see he was trembling. "Like I told the others, we don't want any trouble."

Zain smiled – and the boy looked worried. Quinn noted again that the Deslonder really needed to work on his "friendly" face. "There have been others like us?"

The boy's eyes traveled up and down the large Deslonder, even as his slight body remained stiff with tension. "Well, not exactly like you," he conceded. "But like enough. Tall man, had a blond boy with him. They went north if you're looking for them – even though I told them not to go. We're expecting the Final Storm any day now. It's not a good time."

"Final Storm?"

"The last storm of winter," coughed the boy, who looked very unwell to Quinn. "Not a good idea to be out on the water when it arrives. You should probably head south."

Quinn filed away the information about Dolan as the boy made to shut the door in their faces – only to find its progress barred by the sizeable boot wedged in it.

"Young master," said Zain, pleasantly enough, though with a hint of steel beneath. "We are tired and we are hungry. We are in need of stores to replenish our boat and a good night's sleep on a bed that doesn't have fleas."

The boy shook his head, anxiously. "We've only enough stores for ourselves, and as for beds without fleas . . ." He broke into a shrill laugh – before stopping suddenly, head cocked to one side as though listening to someone inside. Quinn was beginning to think the boy was a bit mad, particularly when his face changed again, this time into a bright smile.

"Look," he said, "you seem like a reasonable lot. I'll see what I can do about some stores, and maybe you can help with cutting some firewood in return?"

Zain stared. "Are you here on your own?"

The boy nodded, shifting from foot to foot. "Um, yes," he said. "There's no one else here at the moment."

"Who lives here?" asked Zain.

"Northern settlers," said the boy, biting his bottom lip. "My parents came with a group . . . well, they washed in here in the Big Storm years ago, and here we've all stayed."

"Where are the rest?"

The boy sighed, and Quinn noticed that he was no longer looking them in the eye. "Not here at the moment . . ." he repeated, then started suddenly, almost as though he'd been struck by a thought or poked from behind. Quinn had never met a stranger kid.

"Look, are you coming in or not?" The boy stood back to open the door wider. Quinn took a step towards the threshold – the boy was weird, but he was more than ready to get out of the biting cold – and was stopped by Zain's big hand on his shoulder.

"Not now," said the Deslonder. "We will return once we have secured our ship."

Quinn was puzzled – and frustrated. This was the closest he'd been to a warm fire in months. What was going on?

The boy's face turned red. "No, no, you must come in. I insist."

Zain was backing away, pushing the crew behind him.

"We shall return later," he said.

The boy's face crumpled, his anger deflating as quickly as it had risen up. He stepped forward, as though about to say something, but then seemed to think better of it and closed the door with a click. Seconds later, they heard the bolt tumble into place.

"Quickly, back to the ship," said Zain, taking off down the icy street at a run.

"What the —?" Quinn followed, with the rest of the confused crew.

"He is not alone in there," hissed Zain as he ran. "Something is not right. His change of mood was too abrupt."

Quinn shook his head. The boy had behaved strangely, it was true. But surely being on your own in a place like this would make anyone strange? Besides . . . "Just remind me why we're running back to the ship then?" he asked. "We still need supplies, no matter who might be in there."

Zain didn't even turn his head. "We need arms," he said. "Knives will not be enough." He increased his speed as they reached the icy jetty, racing lightly down its smooth, slippery surface.

Quinn and the crew followed at a more cautious speed. Who did Zain think was behind the door?

"Zain!" he shouted at the captain's retreating back. "There are no other ships here. Just us."

Zain skidded to a halt at the gangplank to the *Libertas*. "Things are not always as they seem," was all he would say.

Once on board, he ordered the crew to hide everything of value. The *Libertas* was equipped with various false panels and fake floorboards for this very purpose, though the crew laughed at the suggestion. "Like what?" they joked. "Our hammocks?"

Quinn knew that Zain had a special place for his own valuables, though no one on board but Zain knew exactly where that was.

"Gather all your notes together," the captain told him. "Bring them to my cabin."

A strange request, but Quinn hastened to obey. He had not been inside Zain's cabin before, but was not surprised to find that it was similar to his own. Odilon's cabin, he remembered, had been a lush haven of velvets and silk, with every comfort imaginable and walls hung with tapestries for warmth and quiet.

The only difference between Zain's cabin and Quinn's was the size of the bed, which took up more than half the available floor space. A desk was squeezed into one corner, and that was it. Bare floorboards, nothing on the walls.

"Right, out you go," he told Quinn. "If you don't see where I put these, you won't be able to tell under torture."

Quinn gulped and retreated to the deck. *Torture?* What exactly did Zain think was going to happen here?

Zain appeared back up on deck within minutes.

"Ash!" She presented front and center. "You stay on board."

Her face fell.

"You must man the mooring lines," he said. "Be ready to pull them in and push off the minute we get back – or if it looks as though we won't."

She paled, but nodded determinedly.

"Ajax," he said to the redhead, who inclined his head in response. "You're on the mainsail."

"Won't you need me if there's a fight?"

"Probably," conceded Zain. "But I need you here more."

Ajax nodded dejectedly.

"Cleric Greenfield." The old man stepped forward. "You need to stay with the ship," he said. "But stay at the bow and watch closely. You are our witness for the King."

"I shall do my best," he said.

"Abel!"

The crewman rolled his eyes. "Don't say it," he said. "I'm here, at the tiller, right?"

"Right," said Zain. "You're still not up to speed with those injuries and I need someone I can trust. If you see us coming, or anyone else, prepare to launch as soon as Ash here drops the lines."

"We're expecting trouble then," said Abel, raising a smile from Zain.

"More than likely," was the laconic response. "The rest of you, gather your weapons. We're going visiting."

As he watched the crew strap on swords, secrete knives in their breeches and test bows and arrows (Ison and Dilly), Quinn would have given anything for just a knife. He was faced with the choice of going to ask Ash for her kitchen knife again, or being unarmed in what Zain obviously thought was going to be a battle.

But then Zain took him aside.

"I have something for you," he said, producing from behind his back the curved dagger that Ash had used to free them from the tribal village.

"For me?" Quinn took the knife and held it in his hand. "I don't know how to use a curved blade."

Zain raised an eyebrow. "It's a knife," he said. "If someone comes near you, stick it in them! Otherwise, keep out of the way."

"Good point!"

"Something like that," said Zain, grimacing at the lame attempt at a joke. "Right then, let's go. Watch each other's backs. And fronts, for that matter."

With that, he was gone, down the gangplank and hurrying back towards the big ice building. As Quinn rushed after him, he noticed that there was no longer smoke pouring out of the central chimney.

Maybe the boy really did just need someone to cut him some firewood.

Chapter Thirteen

"What do we do now?" Quinn whispered.

"Why are you whispering? We've just run up to the front door, bearing arms, and bashed on it loudly," said Zain loudly, amused even in this tense situation.

"I don't know," Quinn whispered back. "The occasion seems to warrant it."

Zain didn't bother to respond.

"Jericho! Cleaver! Around the back – see if there's another entrance."

They hurried off as fast as the piles of snow around the building would let them. Now there were just five of them at the front door.

Zain thudded on the heavy door again. Quinn fancied he could hear the sound echo around inside.

Suddenly, they heard a faint shout from behind the building.

"This way!" Zain was off again, plowing into the snow and racing towards the yelling, which was growing louder.

Turning a corner, they found a fierce battle in progress. Jericho and Cleaver were fighting desperately against four dark-haired men, swords flashing in the pale sunlight, drops of blood red against the snow.

Zain let out a bloodcurdling cry and leapt into the fray, swinging his huge sword left and right, the three other crew members following.

Quinn stood back, hand on his knife, adhering to Zain's advice that he keep out of the way.

It took only minutes. With superior numbers – and Zain counted for two, thought Quinn – the Verdanians were simply too strong for their opponents and when Jericho thrust his sword through the stomach of their leader, the other three made a run for it, chased by Cook and Cleaver.

They returned a few minutes later, breathing heavily. "They disappeared down the street," puffed Cleaver. "Away from the port."

"Away, you say," said Zain, deep in thought, as he rolled the dead man over. A quick search through his pockets revealed a sharp little dagger and a miniature portrait of a black-haired woman with a red rose in her hair.

"Here," said Zain, handing the dagger to Quinn. "Another for your collection."

He straightened the man's clothing and then stood.

"He's Gelynion," he said. "And he's not alone. Question is, why is he here – and why attack us?" He strode to the back door of the building, pushing it open easily. "Come," he said.

Quinn and the others followed, Quinn very much hoping that the four Gelynions they'd fought had been the only Gelynions in the building. They entered a small room, containing nothing but another door.

"A weather lock," Zain explained, when Dilly commented on the diminutive space. "The two doors are never opened at the same time, which means that drafts don't enter the building."

He pushed open the interior door, and they found themselves in a large, empty room. A desk was placed on one wall, and rows of seats were arranged around the other three. Three doors led from the room.

"It's the harbormaster's room," said Jericho, pointing out a ledger and a pair of brass scales on the desk.

"Hello!" shouted Zain.

There was no answer. The boy they'd met at the front door seemed to have vanished.

"Check for a side office," Zain told them. "And look for the jail. The harbormaster always has a jail."

Quinn grabbed the handle of the closest door, pushing it open.

And stepped back in horror.

~

Ash was bored. Hanging about the ship, holding ropes just in case something might happen, was not her idea of a good time. Not when Quinn was in the heart of the action, whatever that action might be.

She knew that Zain was trying to protect her. He'd told her that he had a daughter her age back in Verdania, under the King's "protection," so he couldn't help but feel fatherly towards her.

All well and good, but Ash had never had a da. Her own had been killed in a hunting accident before she was born, and her mother had chosen to live her life on the edge of the forest. Ash hadn't been brought up to be "protected."

"Couldn't we just go and have a look?" she called out to Ajax, who was busily straightening the lines to the mainsail.

He stopped fiddling and looked at her. "Zain told us to stay here," he said.

"Yes, but . . ."

"Zain told us to stay here," he repeated.

Ash sighed. Ajax had a serious case of hero worship when it came to Zain. He was forever banging on about how fair Zain was, how much he knew, how amazing the training they were getting was . . .

She knew he was right. But that didn't mean she didn't get sick of hearing about it.

She was also sick, it had to be said, of pretending to be a boy. She couldn't see why Zain couldn't just tell the crew she was a girl and be done with it. She'd been on board for months now and nothing bad had happened. Briefly, a fleeting memory of that huge white thing rising up out of the ocean flitted across her brain, but she suppressed it. That had nothing to do with her, surely?

She stamped her feet, trying to get some warmth back into them. She had never been so cold in her entire life. It was the kind of chill that crept under your blankets while you slept, infected your bones and then never entirely left, no matter how many layers of clothing you tried to bury it in. Her nose was red raw, her eyes streamed and her breath hung in a mist about her.

She sighed, looking about for any signs that the crew was returning.

A dark shape appeared behind the small cluster of white buildings.

She blinked. Where had that come from?

As she watched, mouth open, it moved, breaking out from cover and advancing swiftly across the snow.

It was a ship!

"Ajax! Ajax!" she shouted.

He looked up.

"There's a ship! There!" She pointed towards the shore.

"Don't be daft," he said, staring at her. "That's land, you fool."

"Look!" she screamed, watching in amazement as the ship continued to sail across the landscape, parallel to the port.

"Leif's boots!" he cursed, coming to stand beside her. "How can that be?"

Her eyes searched the shoreline desperately. "I don't know," she said. "But we must tell Zain."

"Tell him what? There's a ghost ship sailing on land?"

"That's no ghost! Look at it!"

Now that it was fully in view, they could see the sleek, dark shape of a large, four-masted ship. It was bigger than any of the Verdanian ships, was painted black, and flew no colors.

"We have to tell Zain," she repeated, turning to run down the gangway.

"You stay here," said Ajax, grabbing her arm. "I'll go."

"No!" she shouted, shaking him off. "You're bigger than I am and you need to man the sail. I'll be back as quick as I can." There was no way she was going to be left on board again. This was her sighting, her ship – whatever it was – and she would tell Zain.

In a flash, she was gone, making her way along the slippery ice path as quickly as she could.

As she ran, her mind sped through the facts of what she was seeing.

A ship. On land.

This was not possible.

And yet it was there.

How could it be possible? What could *make* it possible?

Her eyes once again scanned the shoreline, and that's when she saw it. Over to the far right, well beyond the town, such as it was. A change in the color of the shore.

She narrowed her eyes. It was a small break in the shoreline, not much wider than the *Libertas*. She had noticed the darker color before, but thought nothing of it, assuming it was a patch of rocks. But now she could see that the darkness was caused by the water. It did not stop at the white ice as it did everywhere else along the shore. It went past it.

It could mean only one thing.

"An opening," she said out loud. "A channel that goes up behind the town. But how?"

She slid to a stop outside the big building that had been Zain's destination. Where were they?

She pushed hard at the front door. Nothing.

Footprints led down the side of the building. She looked at them carefully. Living in the forest had taught her a few things about tracking. At least five people had gone that way, one large and heavy, the rest lighter. Good enough for her.

At the back of the building, she found a dark-haired man lying on churned-up snow stained red by his blood.

A quick glance reassured her that it was no one she knew. Footprints led in two directions – three sets away from the building, a larger group towards it.

She was pondering which direction to take when she felt a sudden movement behind her. She was turning to meet it, when something crashed into the side of her head, turning the world red.

She crumpled to the freezing ground, unable to even cry out. All she could see through a foggy haze were heavy black boots.

Then one of those boots connected with her face and she knew no more.

~

Quinn was sweating. No mean feat given the temperature outside. But it wasn't heat causing the water to run down his face.

It was fear.

And he had good reason to be afraid.

Shut inside a dark cupboard, which was bolted from the outside, with a body for company? That's what he called good reason to be afraid.

Add to the fact that he had no idea what had happened to Zain and the others, and no reason to imagine that anyone would find him trapped in here, and the case for fear was open and shut.

"Think Quinn, think," he muttered to himself.

Unfortunately, his thought process seemed to have run for the hills as soon as he'd opened this cupboard in the first place.

Inside was the biggest Deslonder he'd ever seen. He made Zain look like a normal-sized person, which was no mean feat.

The Deslonder had his arm around the throat of the boy who'd opened the door to them earlier. As Quinn watched, he lifted his arm and the boy's feet left the ground, his face turning blue and his eyes popping out as his neck took all the strain.

"Zain!"

At Quinn's cry, his captain had come running – and stopped dead.

"Morpeth," Zain said, managing to sound unsurprised. "We meet again."

The huge man stepped out of the cupboard, dragging the boy with him.

"Zain," he said, nodding his head, quite as if the two of them had met on the street. "I heard you might turn up."

Quinn's mouth dropped open. How did these two know each other? Where had the huge man come from?

Zain raised one eyebrow. "Interesting," he said. "I presume then, that we have you to thank for that massacre down the coast."

Morpeth preened a little. "Well, not just me. There are a few of us. Waste of time that whole exercise was. We spent days in that godforsaken hole, thinking they'd have useful information but there was nothing. They seemed to take nothing useful from the land but the blue stone they tore from its wretched grip to build that poor excuse for a castle."

Quinn and Zain exchanged looks. Quinn was grateful that his rudimentary knowledge of Deslondic was keeping up with the conversation. Who was the "us" Morpeth was talking about?

The boy began sputtering, trying to get someone's attention, kicking his feet, which still dangled inches above the floor.

"Drop him," said Zain, giving him a cursory glance. "He is of no interest to you."

"Ah, I see you have met Kurt," Morpeth said. "Kurt is actually of great interest to me, Zain. Great interest. It is he who has shown us through every nook and cranny of this bizarre outpost, sharing all its secrets, even as his parents' bodies lie in the dungeons beneath our feet."

Kurt's head dropped farther at Morpeth's words, cutting off what little air was getting down his throat, and Quinn began to think that his shame would kill him. Zain obviously thought so, too.

"Lift your head, boy!" he shouted in Suspite. Kurt was so startled he did so, still gasping for air.

"Bah, why bother yourself with him?" asked Morpeth, looking at the miserable boy dangling from his hand. "He hid when we arrived and we found him cowering in his own father's office. The harbormaster's son. What a fine specimen he is. He has been translating all his father's records for us. Very helpful he is when it comes to saving his own skin."

Quinn stared. He could not imagine helping the people who had killed not only his parents, but the other members of his community. Then again, anyone faced with Morpeth would have some hard thinking to do . . .

"Ah, Morpeth, you and I both know that people will go to great lengths when their skin is on the line," Zain said, quietly. "Have you not done the same thing?"

"Bah, do not presume to place me in the same category as this poor excuse for a boy," said Morpeth, anger clouding his face. "You know nothing of me. Not anymore."

But he dropped Kurt to the floor, where he proceeded to roll about, clutching his throat and coughing. Everyone ignored him.

"I am sorry you are here, in a way," said Morpeth. "It will not end well for you."

"You are with the Gelynions," Zain stated, ignoring the threat. "It is a good match for you. What I can't figure out is why you, or they, are here."

Quinn couldn't understand what was going on. The tension in the room was very real, and yet these two were chatting away politely.

"I work for Juan Forden," said Morpeth.

Quinn couldn't believe his ears. The legendary Gelynion explorer was here. But that meant . . .

"He has been sent to map the world," continued Morpeth. "We heard about your little race – Eowan Forrest, the Verdanian spy, told us all about it." Zain's only reaction to the name was a flicker of the eye, but Quinn could see Morpeth register it. "Oh yes, the Duke of Forrest. He was such a nice-looking man. Before our inquisitors were finished with him . . . One really should avoid spying as a career if one is determined to keep one's looks, don't you think?"

Quinn could almost see Zain's mind ticking over as he took in this information.

"Our ruler, Rey Bernardino, will not let you be first," said Morpeth. "Juan Forden will return to Gelyn, with the only map. By whatever means necessary."

"Well, then," said Zain, casually. "We have a race on our hands."

Morpeth laughed, a deep, booming sound with no humor in it. "Ha! Had a race perhaps. But your race is over. Come!" The last word was shouted and accompanied by a resounding hand clap.

Shadows moved from alcoves, doors opened and suddenly the Verdanians were surrounded.

"Ha!" Morpeth shouted again, clapping his hands together once more in a gesture that was strangely childlike in one so big. "Got you!"

And indeed they had. Fifteen or more Gelynions stood, swords, daggers, knives and sticks at the ready, in a circle around Quinn and the others. He moved closer to Zain, more for comfort than for anything else.

Zain's hand automatically went to his sword. Three Gelynions drew their weapons.

"No, no, no, no," said Morpeth, shaking his head. "Nothing silly now, Zain. I would hate to have to kill you. Actually . . ." He stopped as though thinking. "Ha! No, I wouldn't," he continued, chuckling to himself. "But not yet. Besides, Juan Forden will want to speak with you."

He turned to the Gelynion soldier standing closest to him. "Take them down to the jail," he ordered. "But not that one."

He pointed directly at Quinn, who did his best to appear unfazed. Inside, his heart, already beating fast, kicked into overdrive.

"That one stays here."

"Why him?" asked Zain, deceptively calm, even as three Gelynion soldiers grabbed his arms and made to drag him off.

"Insurance," said Morpeth. "If you don't go quietly, I'll cut his throat right here . . ."

Quinn blanched as a Gelynion took hold of his arm, drawing him so close that he could feel the heat rising from that huge body.

"And, of course, there's the fact that he's the youngest one," continued Morpeth, as though talking to himself. "That makes him the mapmaker."

Zain raised his eyebrows. "You're very well informed."

"Oh, you'd be surprised," said Morpeth, grinning, his enormous cheeks ballooning up to almost cover his eyes. "Forrest was very, very helpful. Queen Imperia was almost sorry to have to use him as the prey for one of her hunts. But then, she does love her blood sports."

"He'll be no use to you," said Zain, sighing theatrically. "He's hopeless. Forgets everything."

Quinn took that on board, trying not to react.

"Well, I'm not surprised," said Morpeth. "We thought the whole scheme was cracked from the start. Why you'd trust the youth of today with something so huge . . . Not like our day, eh, Zain?"

Quinn nearly rolled his eyes.

"Not at all," said Zain, throwing a hard look at Quinn.

This time Quinn did roll his eyes. He got the message. He'd tell them nothing. Zain didn't need to labor the point.

"Right then, down to the dungeon," said Morpeth, as though organizing a tea party.

As the other crew members were marched out, Quinn wanted desperately to follow them. The dungeon didn't sound like fun, but at least he wouldn't be alone down there.

"So," said Morpeth, "the little mapmaker. Juan Forden will talk to you first."

Quinn said nothing, trying to look unconcerned.

"In the meantime," Morpeth continued, as he patted Quinn down, finding and removing both his knives in seconds, "you'll wait in here. I don't want you concocting some story with Zain."

Quinn briefly considered trying a few of Zain's fighting moves on Morpeth, but quickly discarded the idea. The notion of being able to bring this mountain down with a foot sweep or a flick of the wrist was laughable. Besides, he'd probably had the same training as Zain . . .

That thought wasn't even finished before he found himself unceremoniously hoisted from his feet and shoved backward into the open cupboard. He landed like a sack of potatoes on the cold stone floor, and lay there, dazed. Within seconds, a weight landed on him and he knew that Kurt had been flung in on top of him – he heard a sound like a squashed melon as the Northern boy's head hit the floor. Then the door was shut, the key turned, and the darkness absolute.

"I'll be back as soon as I find Forden," Morpeth said from the other side of the door. "Make yourselves comfortable."

His laughter rang in Quinn's ears long after his heavy tread had left the room.

Now Quinn sat in the dark, fighting the fear, feeling the blackness surround him like a clammy cloak. He'd wiggled out from under the unresponsive Kurt, then done his best to ensure the other boy was lying in a comfortable position. Quinn couldn't even cover him, nor put a makeshift pillow under his head, because to do so would have meant removing one of his own layers – and Quinn knew that the cold could kill him before Forden even got to him.

Which reminded him. He needed to move. He stood up and began stomping on the spot, warming up his feet, which had already begun to cramp. If he managed to escape, he'd need to be able to walk . . .

He laughed out loud, the sound dull in the tiny space. If he managed to escape? Who was he kidding? The door in front of him was solid wood, with a huge lock holding it firmly in place. Quinn wasn't sure what had been in the cupboard in the past, but it had obviously been valuable, judging by the security. Now he felt around, trying to find something, anything, he could use to get out.

Nothing.

The sound of Kurt's shallow breaths filled the cupboard. At least the boy was alive, though Quinn was worried that he wouldn't be for long. Perhaps he had something useful in his pockets . . . A quick pat down revealed that Kurt had nothing but some lint and a feather, which felt soft and delicate beneath Quinn's fingers. It was probably lovely, but not much use as an escape tool. He wondered what color it was.

Sighing, he stood, slipping the feather in his own pocket to examine later. As he did so, his fingers touched something hard, tucked right into the corner. His mam always double stitched the corners of her boys' pockets, making them very durable – but a nightmare for getting things caught in.

Quinn poked and prodded at the object with his fingers, finally pulling it free. As his hand closed around it, he realized it was the animal tooth he'd picked up at the tribal village. Long, pointed, hard.

His mind raced. How could he use this to get out of this black hole? There could only be minutes before Morpeth returned with Forden. If he could escape, he might be able to find the dungeon and get the others.

Quinn approached the door again, distinctive only due to the thin layer of light visible at the bottom. He ran his hands over it again. There were the crossbeams. There was the well-constructed paneling. There was the solid lock. There were the hinges.

Even as he thought the word, his mind brought forth a perfect image of Ajax showing him how to unscrew the hinges to open the bathroom door at the castle. Would the tooth do the job?

Working by feel, anxious sweat now pouring from his brow, he located the small nubs that indicated the iron screws. His fingernails found the slot in the middle and then, praying to anyone who might be listening, he inserted the point of the tooth in the slot and twisted.

Nothing.

Cursing, he tried again, pressing the tooth harder into the screw to give it more grip.

It moved! Wanting to cheer and dance and perhaps even sing a little, Quinn kept twisting until the screw fell out. Ajax had told him to keep the screws so that he could put the door back in position, but he felt that the current circumstances called for speed, not stealth.

It took him more than a few minutes to locate the other five screws and remove them all. Then it was a simple matter of lifting the wrong side of the door away from the jamb as much as he could – it didn't swing as a normal door would, he noted, as the lock definitely didn't have as much give as a hinge did. Slipping out into the harbormaster's office, he made to run down the hall, following in the crew's footsteps, but noticed a large velvet tablecloth draped over the harbormaster's desk. He grabbed it, slipped back into the cupboard, covered Kurt, who still lay huddled on the floor, breathing shallowly, and ran out again.

He hoped it would be enough to keep the boy warm.

Now it was just a matter of finding the others and heading back to the ship.

Before Morpeth and Forden discovered his escape.

The thought of that was enough to make Quinn run even harder.

Chapter Fourteen

Ash heard them coming before she saw them. She quickly closed her eyes, pretending to be passed out or worse. She wasn't sure how long she'd been drifting in and out of consciousness, but she needed to move soon or her body would be frozen in this position forever. At least the snow helped to numb the pain in her face . . .

One pair of feet had lumbered past her earlier, when she'd been incapable of moving, and now several pairs were returning, just as she was beginning to think she might summon up the energy to go.

She opened her eyes slightly, just enough to give her a view of what was going on. Fortunately – if there was anything fortunate about her situation – she'd fallen facing the door to the harbormaster's building, so she could see the group of men disappear inside. She frowned. The men were clad in long, swirling cloaks of burgundy velvet. Showy, but surely not practical in this weather?

One thing was certain – they were not from the *Libertas*, which meant they were more than likely with whomever it was that had hit her. Which meant it was time for her to move.

She held still a minute longer, straining her ears to hear any other footsteps. Nothing. Just the keening wind blowing over the snow and a strange, creaking noise, low and deep. She frowned again, trying to place the sound. It seemed to come from within the very ground itself.

Definitely time to move.

Gingerly, she sat up, stretching her neck to ease the cold, kinked muscles and feeling the back of her head. A goose egg had risen where she'd been hit. At least her mind still seemed to be working. She'd seen her mother work with men who didn't know their own names after being struck on the head.

Getting slowly to her feet, she caught sight of her reflection in the highly polished brass plate on the back door. And winced. Half her face was a motley shade of purple and green with a ring of black rising in the center. No wonder her vision was blurred – she was seeing out of only one eye.

She pushed the back door open and stepped inside. If those men were hurrying into the building, there must be something interesting in here. She could only hope that would be Zain, Quinn and the other Verdanians.

~

If Quinn were compiling a list of his least-favorite things in the world, dark, confined spaces would be at the top. Given that he had just escaped one, he was less than thrilled to find himself wandering lost through another.

He'd followed the path that Zain and the others had taken, out the door of the office, down a hall to some narrow, winding stone stairs, and then gone down, down, down them. At the bottom, in pitch-black darkness, was what he could only assume was the dungeon. He'd called out, but all he could hear was his own voice echoing back at him – which made him realize that this dark void was much larger than he'd imagined.

And so he'd started following a narrow stone path that slanted only downward, one foot in front of the other, hands out like he was playing blindman's buff, bouncing from one cold stone wall to the other. He was getting better at being in the dark, able to sense the emptiness that signified an opening, but he had a horrible feeling that he was walking around in circles.

"Hee-lll-ooo!" he called at intervals, hoping against hope that there were no random Gelynions wandering about down here. At last he heard a faint cry, a "hallo" in response, and he knew he was on the right track. Calling again, he followed the sound, walking deeper and deeper into the dark, relieved when the shouting and hammering grew louder.

Finally, after what felt like an hour but was probably mere minutes, he stopped. He could hear hammering and shouting. He felt the wall. Stones. Stones. Stones. A thick, wooden door.

"Zain?" he whispered, wondering why when the others had been making so much noise. "Is that you?"

"Of course, it's me!" came the loud response from the other side. "Why are you whispering?"

"Um . . ."

"Never mind. You need to get us out of here! And fast! Those Gelynions will be back with Forden within minutes."

"Er, okay." How was he supposed to spring them from a dungeon cell, in the pitch-black, without a . . . Wait a minute.

He felt around the door once again, creeping across from the hinges to where he thought the lock should be. And there it was. A key. The Gelynions had clearly not imagined anyone would be looking for the Verdanians.

He turned the key and pulled open the door.

"Well done!" said Zain, barreling into him in the dark. "I have no idea how you escaped that cupboard and now is not the time, but I've never been so happy to see you. Or not see you, as the case may be."

The others all laughed and agreed.

"Come, we must go," said Zain.

Making their way back proved easier. Quinn had worked out that the passage sloped down and around, like a spiral. It was disorientating, but there was basically only one way in – and one way out.

Zain and the others had been down there long enough for their eyes to adjust, so they soon overtook him and were at the bottom of the stairs in no time.

"We need to get back to the ship as fast as we can," said Zain. "I'm only hoping we're not too –" He stopped suddenly and held up his hand. In the silence, above his own beating heart, Quinn could hear trampling feet.

"They're coming!" said Zain. "Ison, Dilly – you two are the fastest, run as fast as you can up those stairs and back to the ship. Abel, Ash and Ajax will need help. Leave a wide trail and make as much noise as you can – I want them to think we've all escaped."

Dilly and Ison didn't even stop to nod.

"The rest of you, prepare to fight," said Zain, grimly. Quinn began to sweat again, as they waited in the dark.

Sure enough, they soon heard shouts of surprise overhead, then running feet.

"There are four running, two following," said Zain. "Morpeth is following – I can hear his heavy step – probably with Forden. The other four will, most likely, be sailors."

"The door is open! You two, after them!" The order,

shouted in Gelynion, came from an authoritative voice that Quinn didn't recognize. Forden!

Thick boots stomped overhead. "You two, downstairs. Check if anyone's there."

"They're coming," said Quinn.

"You understand them?" asked Zain.

"Some," Quinn answered. He felt the Deslonders around him tense, ready for action, and tried to remember everything Zain had taught him.

The first Gelynion appeared at the bottom of the stairs, backlit by the faint light from above and, with his eyes still adjusting, he didn't even see Jericho step out from the shadows. Within seconds, he was on the floor, landing heavily on his side as Jericho knocked his feet out from under him. The breath left his body in a whoosh and he lay still, winded and unconscious from his fall.

The crew made light work of the other sailor, and soon they were both lined up neatly to one side of the stairs. Then they waited.

Quinn heard two sets of footsteps arrive at the top of the stairs.

"Alessandro?" Morpeth's voice was cautious.

No reply.

"Something has happened," the big Deslonder said. "I cannot hear their footsteps."

Just then one of the Gelynions rolled and called out.

A quick kick from Jericho silenced him, but the damage was done.

"Bah!" said Forden. "We have no time for this. Get down there and find out what's going on. I will guard the exit with my sword."

There was a silence. "The others will be with us soon," said Morpeth. "We can send them down for the mapmaker."

"We don't even know if he's there." There was the sound of pacing overhead.

"Why don't we rush up and attack them?" Quinn whispered to Zain. "There are only two of them and they can't decide what to do."

"They have the higher ground and weapons," said Zain. "And one of them is Morpeth. What would the win cost us? We need every hand to man the *Libertas*. We'll wait here – our eyes are adjusted to the dark and we have the advantage."

Quinn sighed, listening hard once more.

Forden was speaking again. "Are you scared of a few Verdanians?" he asked Morpeth softly, his voice low and mean.

"I am scared of nothing," roared Morpeth, and Quinn heard the swoosh of metal as he drew a sword. "I will kill them with Zain's own sword if they are there."

"He's coming down," said Quinn, quietly. "With your sword."

Next to him, Zain stood taller. "Steady now," he

whispered to Cleaver, Cook and Jericho. "Our best hope is surprise."

Slowly, steadily, Morpeth's tread came closer as, step-by-step, he descended into the dark. Remembering the size of Zain's huge sword, Quinn felt his knees begin to quake.

Beside him, he could hear Zain whisper to the crew, though he couldn't hear what they said, and the men began to move silently, farther into the shadows, flanking either side of the stairs. One large hand on Quinn's shoulder pushed him into position behind Cleaver, who, Quinn noticed, had removed his cloak and was holding it in one hand.

Seconds later, he realized that the other end of Cleaver's cloak was in Jericho's hand, stretched across to the other side of the stairwell. Morpeth's tread got louder and the faint light coming from the mouth of the stairwell was blocked as his bulk moved closer.

Shrinking into the cold stones of the passageway, Quinn could see the silhouette of the huge sword Morpeth held aloft and wondered just how long they would stand here, waiting to die. A few more steps and Morpeth would stand on them in the dark.

"Now!" shouted Zain. Jericho and Cleaver jerked the cloak upward and Morpeth crashed to the ground between them, the sword clattering on the stone floor. Zain didn't wait to find out what state the Deslonder was in, reaching down to pull the sword from his hand.

“Are you going to kill him?” Quinn asked, as Cleaver pulled his cloak out from underneath Morpeth and snuggled into it.

Zain’s teeth flashed white in the dark. “Oh no,” he said. “I want him to live with the shame of this moment for a while first.”

Again, Quinn wondered about the history between these two.

“Quickly now,” said Zain. “Behind me. Forden awaits us up there.”

With a roar, he charged up the stairs, huge sword held overhead. Only to stop dead at the top. Quinn, following close behind, blinking in the light, ran into him with an *oof*.

The room was empty.

“Ha! He must have heard Morpeth fall, and didn’t stick around to see what happened next,” chortled Jericho.

“Or he’s decided that our ship is more valuable than we are,” said Zain. “We must get back to the *Libertas*.”

“The door is locked!” said Quinn, rattling the handle. “And I smell something burning.” Even as he spoke, smoke began seeping under the door. Quinn looked around at the walls of ice, the floors of stone . . . and the wood paneling that lined the room.

They’d escaped the dungeon only to become trapped in a burning building!

Chapter Fifteen

"Will it melt before it burns us?" asked Quinn, hopefully.

Zain looked at him balefully. "I don't intend to wait around to find out," he said.

"Look!" said Jericho. "That handle's turning."

And so it was. The door that he had tried was being rattled from the outside. The Verdanians looked at each other. Had it been a hoax? Was this Forden coming back for a second try?

They heard the key turn and Jericho assumed the fighting stance, ready to take down whomever stepped through the door.

The door pushed slowly open.

"Hello," said Ash. "Fancy meeting you here."

Quinn stared at her. Her face was swollen and stained a peculiar color, but he'd never been happier to see her.

"This way!" she said, turning to leave. "That other lot went out the back door, so I think we should go out the front."

"We should get Kurt," Quinn said to Zain. He hadn't liked much about the Northern boy, but couldn't leave him to die either. "And what about Morpeth? Are you going to leave him down there?"

"Morpeth will take care of himself," said Zain. "He usually does. But you and Jericho go and get the boy. We'll wait until the count of fifty for you, no longer." With that, he began counting and Jericho and Quinn hared off down the hallway to the cupboard. They were back as Zain counted forty-eight, with Kurt slung over Jericho's strong shoulders like a side of beef.

"Let's go!" shouted Ash, and they hurried after her.

"By the way, what are you doing here?" Zain asked her as they ran. "I left you on the ship."

She grinned, or grimaced, Quinn wasn't sure which. "I came to tell you about the ghost ship," she said. "And stayed to save your bacon."

Quinn sputtered. "Save our bacon! I'd already saved them once!"

She cast him a sidelong glance, even as she ran. "I'd say your bacon looked nearly cooked in there."

He managed a laugh. She was probably right and it felt so good to be out in the open again that he was happy to let her have the point.

"What's this about a ghost ship?" asked Zain, as they approached the ice jetty and began the slippery slide out to the ship.

"Over there!" she shouted, pointing to the left – towards land.

Quinn glanced that way and nearly stopped in amazement.

"I worked out that it was in a channel," Ash was saying. "But when we first saw it, we thought it was sailing on land!"

"I can see why you'd think that," said Zain, staring at the ship. "It's Gelynion, Juan Forden's ship. They had her hidden up behind the village when we arrived."

"Hey!" shouted Jericho from the back of the pack, still lugging Kurt. "We've got company!"

Chancing a quick glance over his shoulder, Quinn could see a pack of Gelynions bearing down on them. How many were on that ship anyway? Ahead of him, he could see another group on the jetty near the *Libertas*, which was drifting away from her moorings.

Dilly and Ison had reached the ship ahead of the Gelynions, hauled up the anchor, and cast off the lines that tethered the ship. Which kept her safe from the Gelynions, who were shouting and waving swords on the jetty, but also kept her out of reach of the desperate Verdanians.

Had they come so far only to end up sandwiched between two packs of Gelynions?

"What are we going to do?" Quinn gasped at Zain.

"Go left," shouted a wavering, unfamiliar voice in Suspite.

Quinn looked at his captain. "Who was that?"

"It's him," shouted Jericho. "The boy."

"Past the jetty," the weak voice continued, barely discernible over the tramping of their feet and the Gelynions' shouting. "Longboat hidden in ice cave. Near canal."

"Come!" shouted Zain, putting on a burst of speed. Reinvigorated with hope, the others followed hard at his heels. Out in the bay, the *Libertas* continued to drift slowly.

~

They never would have found the longboat on their own. The entrance to the ice cave didn't look big enough to fit a man, let alone a boat. But it took only a few seconds of heavy kicking by Zain, Cleaver and Cook to collapse the entrance, and within minutes they were pulling the boat clear and sliding it into the water.

The Verdanians piled in, with Jericho throwing Kurt in, before pushing the boat off the mouth of the canal and into the bay. Zain and Cleaver took the oars and rowed for all they were worth.

The Gelynions reached their casting-off point seconds later and threw knives, and even a sword, at the departing boat in frustration.

"Ajax! Ajax!" Quinn started shouting as the crowded longboat drew near the *Libertas*.

The redhead popped his head over the side, and in one look summed up the situation. "Abel!" Quinn heard him shout. "Hold her steady."

He threw a rope ladder over the side, and soon Zain and Cleaver were positioning the longboat under it. Quinn had never attempted to climb from one boat to another while both were moving, but the thought of the freezing swim that lay at the bottom of the ladder if he missed his footing on the swaying rope was enough to focus his efforts. Ash came up the ladder after him, swift and sure, and Quinn pulled her over the side with relief.

On shore, the two parties of Gelynions had merged, and Quinn could see Forden in the middle of them, waving his arms and shouting in frustration. Smoke billowed to the sky from the harbormaster's building and, as Quinn watched, a huge figure emerged, bent double with coughing. Morpeth had survived, as Zain had predicted.

Jericho landed on deck, a knife in each hand and one in his teeth – Gelynion weapons that had landed in the longboat. He handed them out amongst the crew members, keeping a sword, tucked through his belt, for himself. Quinn couldn't help but lament the loss of his own collection of weapons – he'd gone from no weapons to two weapons and back to none in the space of a few hours.

But at least they were all safe. For now.

Chapter Sixteen

The world was ending. Gazing at the sky, Quinn could feel horror rising up from his toes. The dragon at the end of the world was not a fairy tale. It was real. It was here. And it was breathing fire.

Beside him, Ash took his hand. He had half a thought to throw her off, remembering she was supposed to be a boy, but instead squeezed her fingers tightly. If he was going to be burned to a crisp by a huge, scaly dragon with bad breath, he was going to have the comfort of her friendship.

The sky above them was awash with color. Bright flashes of green and blue, red and purple, infinite nameless shades in between. Reflected on the glassy ocean, they surrounded the *Libertas* and her occupants.

"What is it?" he asked Zain, almost breathless with fear.

"I don't know," admitted the captain, clutching the tiller as he stared upward.

Quinn gulped. "Is it Genesi?" he asked.

Zain looked down at him, eyes blank. "I don't know," he admitted again.

This was the moment of truth, thought Quinn, dropping Ash's hand. In the fairy tale, the dragon awaited at the end of the earth. Anyone foolish enough to venture that far would simply drop off the edge, into his waiting jaws. He was always hungry, always waiting. When he was little, Quinn's brothers used to threaten to send him to Genesi whenever he annoyed them. He'd been terrified. Much as he was now, with the idea of Genesi fast becoming a reality.

"Should we turn around?" he ventured, trying to swallow his panic. "Your family . . ."

Head thrown back, staring up at the heavens, Zain shook his head. "There is no reward without risk," he said, turning to look at Quinn. "Going home because we are scared would be no homecoming. My family would not be free."

Quinn knew what he meant. It was one thing not to win the race, quite another to arrive back in Verdania having given up.

But still . . . "We might all die! Going home without freedom is one thing but having no life at all is quite another!"

Zain stood taller. "Slavery is no life at all," he said, simply. "Besides, Quinn Freeman, do you not also have reason to risk all?"

Quinn thought of going home. To the village he loved, the farm, the cozy, safe world that he'd known, his family . . . His family. The reproach in his father's eyes, the teasing he would face for the rest of his life from his disappointed brothers, the unbearable understanding from his mam . . .

"You're right," he said. "I guess."

"Keep faith, Quinn Freeman," said Zain. "Keep faith. Those flashes are a long way from us. And they are above us. Not below us. Surely if we were going to drop off the world into the mouth of a dragon, they would be below us?"

That made sense.

"Also," Quinn said, thoughtfully, "the ocean is behaving no differently. If anything, it is calmer than usual. Surely if we were going to drop off the end of the world, it would be rushing away from us, towards the horizon?"

"Good point," said Ash. "Like a waterfall."

Zain smiled at them. "That's the way. Look for reasons to keep going, not for reasons to stop."

Ajax came up behind them, overhearing Zain's last words.

"Are we not worried about Genesi?" he asked, fearfully. "Cleric Greenfield is down in his cabin, praying for our souls."

"Good," said Zain. "Always best to cover all angles."

Ajax looked from one to the other, bewildered, as they laughed.

"There's no mention on the Northerners' rug of this," he said, waving his arms around him.

"No," said Quinn, slowly. "But look at him."

He gestured to the deck, where Kurt was huddled beside a mast. He looked miserable and seasick, but he did not look afraid.

"I think he's seen this before," Quinn continued. "Maybe he knows that it only happens sometimes. Maybe it's actually a good sign." He would have gone over and asked Kurt, but so far no one had been able to get two words out of him. After the directions to the ice cave, he'd not said a thing.

"How can this be good?" said Ajax, once again flinging his arms around in alarm.

Ash took his arm to calm him. Or tried to. As she did so, his sudden movement knocked her off her feet and she crashed to the deck in a heap.

"Oh wow," she said, lying on her back. "I see stars."

"And I," said Zain, glancing quickly down to make sure she was all right, before fixing his eyes firmly on the horizon once again, "see a sail."

Quinn didn't need an invitation to shinny up the mast to the lookout platform. From there, against a backdrop of shooting, bouncing light, his sharp eyes could see a four-masted ship, under full sail. He recognized the silhouette.

"It's the *Fair Maiden*," he shouted down to the deck. "We've caught up to Odilon."

~

"You stole my scribe!"

The meeting with Odilon was off to a great start.

"No," said Zain, patiently. "You left him for dead. We picked him up. You should be thanking us for the fact that you have a scribe at all."

"I haven't had one for the past month!" shrieked Odilon, spittle flying from his mouth. Quinn watched, fascinated, as the thin veneer of civilized nobility that he wore cracked open like an egg. "Why didn't you catch up sooner?"

"We, er, ran into some problems," said Zain smoothly, walking farther up the beach. The two ships had moored in a beautiful little bay, fringed with white sand and surrounded by the tallest trees Quinn had ever seen. Their straight red trunks were as round as three cows put together, and disappeared towards the sky. It was only from the ship that you could get a true perspective on their height, and then it was breathtaking.

Quinn was just happy to see the first signs of spring creeping over this bay at the top of the world, tiny green leaves clinging to bare branches, birds darting in and out.

"Anyway," Zain continued, "the point is that he's here now."

Ajax stared stolidly in the distance. When Zain had told him that he'd planned to catch the *Fair Maiden* and return him to Odilon, the big redhead was horrified. "Can't I just stay with you?" he asked. "I've been useful, haven't I?"

"Yes," Zain agreed gently. "But the race is not fair if Odilon has no scribe."

"So?" said Ajax. "You've got twice as much chance of winning."

Zain smiled. "That's not the point."

Quinn was almost as frustrated as Ajax. He liked having his friend on board and would miss him. "You would sail us into those strange lights for freedom, but you won't take an advantage?" Quinn asked, unable to help himself.

"It is not an advantage if it can be used against you at a later time," was all that Zain would say in response. Thinking about it later, Quinn thought he understood. As a slave, Zain had to win in the most scrupulous way possible.

And so the *Libertas* had drawn close enough to the *Fair Maiden* for the message to be given that a meeting was necessary.

Now Ajax stood, carrying the bag that Zain had given him for his drawings, withdrawn and unhappy. Quinn wished he could do something. He would miss the big redhead with his easy smile and quick jokes. And he knew, from what Ajax had told him, that life on board the *Fair Maiden* was not much fun. At least Quinn still had Ash. Ajax had no one his age on board, and was treated like an afterthought by Odilon and the crew.

"Here, boy!" Odilon now said. Quinn saw Zain wince at his tone, but Ajax did as he was told, and trudged after Odilon, walking as though his bag was packed with stone as he made his way down to the longboat.

"Wait!" Ash ran down the beach after him, a pot in her hand. "This is for you!" She gave the pot to Ajax, who looked down at it with little interest, then smiled slightly when he saw what it was. One of Ash's precious plants, now beginning to show the signs of tiny, bright-green fruit.

"Look after it," she said.

"I will," he said, leaning in towards her. Quinn saw him whisper something in her ear and she blushed as red as those tiny fruits would one day be, before turning and fleeing back to Quinn.

"What did he say?" Quinn asked.

"He said that he'd always known I was a girl, even if everyone else on board didn't."

Quinn looked up to find Ajax's eyes on him. Ajax winked, his old playful spark lighting his face for just a moment. But it was quickly gone and he turned once more to the longboat, folding his big frame into the front, not looking back again as the boat left the shore and made its way slowly out to the *Fair Maiden*.

“He’ll be okay.” Zain put one hand each on Quinn’s and Ash’s shoulders.

Quinn nodded, unable to look at Ash, who was sniffing quietly beside him. He wished he were as sure of Ajax’s future as Zain was.

“And now,” said Zain, clapping their shoulders, “we shall scout for any fresh food we can find and then follow them out of the harbor.”

Ash nodded, wiping her eyes. “I will see if I can replenish some of my herb stocks,” she said, looking around the little cove. “There must be something useful here.”

That was Ash, thought Quinn. Ever practical. “I’ll help,” he said, knowing he was committing to standing around in prickly bushes while she crawled about on her hands and knees, muttering to herself. It wasn’t the most fun he’d ever had, but at least it would give him something to do. And it was better than staying on the beach looking after the silent Kurt. Someone else could have that job.

“That’s the boy,” said Zain, loudly. “Onward and upward.”

Both rolled their eyes at his fake cheerfulness. It seemed their adventures in the frozen north had had the effect of thawing out their captain. Or perhaps it was simply that Quinn had a new respect and insight into the man who steered their ship. Either way, there’d been a definite relaxing in the Deslonder’s manner and he’d even become, on occasion, almost chatty.

"Come on," said Ash. "You hold the basket."

Hours later, Quinn was regretting his decision to help. The spring sun shone hot on his bare head and if Ash said "just five more minutes" again, he was going to drop the heavy basket on her head.

"Oh, Quinn, look!"

He looked. Another weedy-looking plant.

"Do you know what this is?" Ash asked, reverently stroking a leaf.

"A plant," he said, irritably.

"It's woad," she said. "The clerics grow it."

"So?"

"So, they use it to make blue ink," she said. "For their books."

That stopped him. "Could we?" he asked, holding his breath. He had a small supply of black ink with which to create his maps, but no colors. Colored inks were too precious – and too unstable – to travel. He knew the color she was talking about – a rich, dark blue. He wanted it.

She paused, thinking, rubbing the leaves between her fingers. "I could try," she said. "I saw it done once when Ma and I were delivering herbs to Cleric Redland. They wrap the leaves into balls and then ferment them."

"Could you do other colors as well?"

"I guess," she said. "We could experiment and see what we can come up with. It depends on what we find in our travels."

"What are we looking for?" he asked, suddenly enthused about this foraging excursion.

"Hmm . . . We might be able to extract brown from bark," she said, walking towards a large oak tree. "Or nutshells, perhaps? I'm pretty sure we can do green from stinging nettles, red from berries . . . I don't know, Quinn. All the plants are so unfamiliar. It'll be trial and error."

He laughed. "Like the rest of this journey, then."

She smiled. "Exactly."

He looked up again at the sun, now high overhead. "We'd best get back," he said. "Zain will want to leave before the sun gets too much higher, or we'll be settling in for the night and giving Odilon an even bigger start on us."

"Oh, forget about Odilon," she said. "We caught him once, we'll catch him again."

Quinn smiled. "Nonetheless, Zain did say not to be too long."

She nodded. "You go ahead. I'll just grab some more woad and some of those red berries over there – I saw some kind of rat eating them before, so they must be okay to eat."

He frowned. "Maybe they're okay for rats but not for us?"

"Maybe," she conceded. "But mostly it goes both ways. If animals are okay with them, we are too. Besides, we might be able to make a red ink out of them."

"All right then," he said. "But don't be long."

Scrambling down the hillside towards the beach, dragging Ash's basket behind him, he was surprised to see another ship in the bay. It seemed that Dolan and Ira had joined the party, though the *Fair Maiden* was long gone.

This would be interesting. Given that the crew from the *Wandering Spirit* had stolen all their food last time they'd met, he couldn't imagine Zain giving them a very friendly reception. Surely even his patience and tolerance would be tested?

But as he drew closer, he could see Zain and Dolan huddled together under a tree while Ira looked on from afar. The men appeared to be comparing notes.

"What are they talking about?" he asked Ira as soon as he drew near enough. The blond boy looked down from his superior height and hesitated.

"What are they talking about?" Quinn repeated, through clenched teeth. Zain might be happy to let bygones be bygones, but Quinn would not easily forgive endless weeks of nothing but gruel to eat.

"Nothing that concerns you," Ira replied, shifting slightly so that his shoulder blocked Quinn's view.

Quinn snorted. He felt surprisingly unafraid of the noble boy. When he thought back to himself shivering naked in a bath in the dark, he wanted to spit. Not any-more. He realized that his time with Zain had given him more than traditional fighting skills – it had given him the confidence to stand his ground *without* having to use them.

And so he did the last thing that Ira expected. He smiled and clapped the older boy on the back.

"We'll see," he said heartily, subconsciously echoing Zain's tone. "We'll see."

Moments later, his confidence was rewarded when Zain turned to him and called him over.

Flashing another quick smile at the disconcerted Ira, he strode over to his captain, giving his cloak an extra flap as he did so.

"Don't get cocky," said Zain, immediately. He missed nothing. "We have a question for you."

He was holding a crude drawing on parchment. It took Quinn just seconds to realize that this must be Dolan's version of the mapped journey and he was gratified to see that it was much less detailed than his own.

"Where was the ice village?" asked Zain. "Point it out."

Quinn dropped a finger on the spot without hesitating.

"No," said Dolan, shaking his head. "It was farther south."

Quinn squinted more closely at the map and opened his mouth to disagree.

"I'm sure you're right," said Zain, kicking his young mapmaker in the ankle. "The boy is young. He must be mistaken."

Quinn bit back a retort. Zain's gentle taps could leave

a person bruised for weeks. "Why do you want to know?" he asked instead.

"Dolan has also had a run-in with the Gelynions," said Zain. "We are trying to work out their current position."

"Where did you see them?" Quinn asked, turning to Dolan. The explorer rolled his eyes at him, not deigning to answer a mere boy.

Zain gave Dolan a pointed look and Dolan sighed, the force of his exhalation lifting his curly hair skyward.

"Here," he said, slapping the point of one dirty finger on the map, leaving a smudge mark that Quinn calculated meant that the *Wandering Spirit* had had to cover a lot more ground than the *Libertas* as she'd drifted much farther east than they had. Did that mean the Gelynions had also lost their way?

Zain hadn't missed it.

"Any particular reason you went so far east?" he asked, politeness personified.

Dolan frowned. "We got hit by a dirty great storm," he growled. "Not far from that godforsaken ice village."

Zain nodded. They too had weathered the storm but, having been forewarned about it by Kurt in that very first meeting with him, they'd taken shelter in a small cove even as its first winds began to make whitecaps on the waves. The Gelynions must have sailed right by them in their pursuit of the *Libertas* and hit the Final Storm head on.

"What do you want from us now?" Zain continued.

"Isn't it obvious?" rumbled Dolan, hands on hips. "We need to band together against those blasted Gelynions."

Quinn's mouth dropped open. The man who had stolen all their food and left them to die in the snow now wanted an alliance. His eyes flew to Zain, hoping that the Deslonder would give Dolan the smack around the chops he deserved.

Instead, Zain was rubbing his own chin thoughtfully, his fingernails making tiny scratch-scratch noises in the stubble.

"We may not see them again," he pointed out.

"Of course we'll see them again! We're on the same course. We're all headed west."

Zain and Quinn exchanged glances. They'd decided the previous evening to follow the coastline farther south before striking west. Zain wanted to get a better idea of the size and scale of land they had discovered. Quinn was happy to go along with it – he wanted to avoid the potentially endless oceans for as long as he could. He felt better with land in sight.

Dolan did not miss the glance. "What?" he said. "What do you know?"

"Nothing," said Zain smoothly. "Nothing at all. Of course you are right, we are all headed in the same direction. And we are countrymen so, of course, we will be allies, watching each others' backs with the Gelynions."

The same forced heartiness was in his tone as when he'd tried to convince Quinn and Ash that Ajax would be okay. Quinn shivered inside. Given the glimpse that they'd already had of Dolan's treachery, he wasn't sure if this alliance wouldn't prove more dangerous than their encounter with Juan Forden. At least Forden made it clear that he was the enemy. Sometimes it was better to know where you stood.

"Excellent," said Dolan, rubbing his hands together. "Then we shall travel together in convoy. Let us compare notes. Ira!"

He turned towards the blond boy, who hurried forward when beckoned, looking extremely unhappy at having been left out so far.

"Show us what you have then," said Dolan, turning back to Zain, who smiled, that familiar baring of teeth that Quinn now knew meant the recipient should start to worry.

"I think not," Zain said.

"But you've already seen ours!" Ira pointed angrily to the map, still in Zain's left hand.

"Yes," said Zain. "But we are under no obligation to share what we know. Just as we *were* under no obligation to share our food with you. You took advantage of that . . . and yet, here we are . . ."

He reached down inside his cloak and pulled out one of the Gelynion daggers that Jericho had rescued from the longboat, making sure that both Ira and Dolan got a good look at the markings. "I suggest we leave it there," Zain continued. "Knowing that we will come to your aid should the Gelynions attack – as you will come to ours."

Ira's eyes widened as he caught the significance of the markings. The *Libertas* had met with the Gelynions and had taken weapons from them. Unlike the *Wandering Spirit*, which had heaved to and raced ahead of the wind to put as much distance between them and the Gelynions as possible.

Dolan's chest puffed up with anger. "An alliance is only as strong as the trust that binds us!" he blustered.

Zain took a step towards him, towering over the smaller man, who reminded Quinn of one of his mother's bantam roosters. "Never forget that we are competitors," he said. "We will fight as Verdanians against the Gelynion threat, but we compete only for ourselves."

Quinn couldn't help it, he smirked – at last! – and then groaned in pain as the heel of Ira's boot came down on his instep. He had no time to dwell on it, nor even to turn and drop the older boy into the sand with a roundhouse kick – Zain was speaking to him.

"I think we have everything we need here, don't we, Quinn?"

Through the tears of pain and rage in his eyes, Quinn caught Zain's look and nodded. He'd memorized Dolan's notes.

Ira laughed. "Nothing's what you need then," he said. "Because nothing's what you've got."

With that, he snatched the document from Zain's hand. "This is mine," he said. "I am the mapmaker and I will take charge of it."

Zain bowed. "Of course," he said. "We wouldn't dream otherwise."

"Right then," said Dolan, shifting nervously on his feet. "We'll be off. Stick close to us. Keep an eye out for those Gelynions. Tally ho!"

With the last cry, his crew rallied around him and they all made their way back down the beach to the waiting longboats.

Shading his eyes against the afternoon sun, Quinn watched them go.

"Can you tell me why we didn't beat them black-and-blue for stealing our food?" he asked.

"Have you ever heard the saying 'Keep your friends close and your enemies closer'?"

Quinn sighed. "Of course, I've heard it," he said. "But it wasn't one that we lived by in Markham. My brothers preferred, 'Keep your friends close and banish your enemies to the fires of Genesi.'"

Zain chuckled. "Also a good saying, but in this case, the true enemy is not Dolan, nor Odilon. We may find we need friends when it comes to Juan Forden, and friends are scarce out here."

Quinn thought about that for a moment. "Okay," he conceded. "I take your point. But can we please stop calling them friends?"

"And what term would you prefer?"

Stumped, Quinn searched the horizon for inspiration. His mind raced at lightning speed, discarding option after option.

"Ah!" he said at last, his grin as wide as the ocean. "I have it."

He paused.

"Well," said Zain, clamping a huge hand on his shoulder. "Don't keep me in suspense. I hate suspense."

Quinn took one small, warm moment to enjoy the new friendship with his captain, before crowing, "Enemends!"

Zain's laughter boomed down the beach, causing heads to turn their way.

"Enemends, it is."

~

Back on board, with the sails full of wind and the gentle splashing sound of waves disappearing under the prow, Quinn stared up at the black velvet of the night sky. When they'd first left Verdania, he'd taken comfort from the fact that the sky he looked at each night on the ship was the same as the one he'd stared up at from the fields of his father's farm.

Now, though, even the stars were different. Had they crossed an invisible line somewhere that took them from their own world to another? Perhaps that was the secret – the great storm they'd all weathered had simply blown them into a different realm. He shifted uncomfortably on the hard wooden deck. If that were the case, would they ever find their way back?

It had been a long day. They'd returned to the *Libertas* with a longboat full of leaves and plants, all collected by Ash. Some for eating, some for creating the inks she was hoping to make for him. He felt his fingers tingle at the idea of colored inks. Only clerics and the very rich could afford them at home. To be able to color his map would surely put it in good contention to win the contest . . . assuming it – and he – got home.

Zain and he had gone straight to the wheelhouse, eager to get the information sitting in Quinn's mind out onto parchment.

And that's when they'd discovered that the treasured tapestry map was gone.

Enemends indeed.

"Dolan!" Quinn had shouted, incensed at the loss of the beautiful object. The knowledge it contained was one thing – and he would never lose that while his memory held together – but he and Ajax had gone through such hardship to gain the tapestry . . .

"I don't think so," said Zain, slowly. "He was nowhere near our ship today."

"His crew then! Ira!"

But Zain was shaking his head, sadly.

"Who else could it be?"

And then he knew. His mind clicked through the images of the day and he remembered Ajax lugging his pack down to the beach, his wink as he'd left.

Ajax had taken the tapestry.

Deflated, Quinn slumped down the wall.

"You don't need it," said Zain, with quiet confidence.

"No. But that's not the point."

"It is entirely the point. Ajax does need it. To go back to Odilon completely empty-handed would have been to enter a fool's contract."

"Why are you so forgiving all the time?" Quinn raged, a hot feeling rising up from his feet to his ears. His voice seemed to come from someone else. Part of him was horrified at daring to shout at Zain, his captain. Another part, the angry, betrayed, hurt part, the part that had never wanted to come on this journey and couldn't believe that he was more miles from home than he could ever have imagined was possible . . . that part was cheering.

Zain sat down beside him. "Many years ago, I was like you," he said.

"Oh, don't start with the 'you will grow up and then you will understand' hogwash," said Quinn. "My brothers have been giving me that my whole life."

Zain smiled. "I would never, er, 'hogwash' you," he said. "I have simply learned through experience that raging at everything expels a lot of energy for little gain. Much better to conserve that rage, to keep it where you need it, so that when the time comes you are three times the man you need to be."

Quinn groaned. "Put up with it, you mean! What kind of attitude is that?"

Zain laughed softly. "You misunderstand. Ride the flow while it is strong and against you. Then channel it when the time is right. There are many things in the world that you cannot change, Quinn. I know. I also know that you can either accept these things, or bash your head against them over and over until they leave you senseless."

"Are you saying that we can't change what Dolan did? What Ajax did?"

"Ajax we will come to in a moment," said Zain. "Dolan, no, we cannot change it. He took our food. That moment is gone. We rise above it for now because it suits us. We change to suit the circumstances. That is what I am trying to say, Quinn. You cannot change what other people will do. You can only change how you react to those things."

Quinn shook his head, weary now that his anger was spent.

"And Ajax?"

"Ajax found that tapestry too," said Zain. "He was as entitled to it as you were. And you don't need it anymore."

"But he didn't know that!" Quinn protested.

"Didn't he?" asked Zain. "He saw you learn a language overnight, Quinn. He has a fair idea of who you are. More, perhaps, than you do."

Quinn couldn't tell Zain how worrying this was for him. Ajax had seen his memory in action – how much would he reveal to Odilon? It was one thing for the *Libertas* crew to know – and even after everything that had happened, Cook and Dilly still wouldn't be alone with him – quite another for the word to spread.

Now, lying under the endless sky, Quinn thought about Zain's words again. It was true that the stars weren't the same but neither, if it came right down to it, was he. Yes, he was still more comfortable with land in sight, but it no longer mattered that it wasn't familiar land. He was, though he'd never admit it to Ash or Zain, excited about what the next stage of the journey might bring – as long as he wasn't meeting Genesi on a downward spiral off the end of the world.

Dragons that may or may not exist, however, took up less of the alarmed space in his head these days than the very real, very human Gelynions.

"Ten bells," called the night watchman, high above him on the mast. "All is well."

Yes, thought Quinn, rolling over to a standing position, it was. He still missed his family and the farm with an ache, but he was comforted by the knowledge that they were all eating well, thanks to him.

A sudden cry from above distracted him from thoughts of his mother's lamb stew with golden dumplings.

"What is it?" he shouted back.

"Monster!"

The Great White Beast. It had to be!

Quinn rushed to the side, peering out into the darkness. He could see nothing in the black waves, just the moon reflecting off the white spray thrown up by the ship.

"There!" shouted Ash, appearing beside him and pointing to port.

Sure enough, there it was, rising high from the water, the huge pointed horn on its head aimed skyward. Seawater rained down on them, and the *Libertas* began rocking frantically back and forth.

"It's going to take us down!" screamed Ash, while Kurt watched on in silent horror. He had, unusually, left his position by the mast to see what all the fuss was about.

"No," said Quinn, serenely. "No. It's good luck for us. I know it."

"How can you say that?"

"I just know."

And he stood there, gazing awestruck at this beast, as tall as the turret on the King's castle, ghostly in appearance.

He could not explain why he was not afraid. He was just glad of it, as all around him the crew rushed blindly hither and thither. Kurt had returned to his station, clutching the mast for all he was worth.

"Hello there," he whispered. "I'm going to name you Nammu." His mother had told him stories of the Goddess of the Sea. It seemed a fitting name for such a magical beast, even if he had no idea if it were male or female.

Nammu arched backward and crashed into the waves, disappearing into the darkness. Within minutes the water around them had settled and they were sailing smoothly south once more.

Zain joined him at the rail. "Ash tells me you believe the white beast brings good fortune," he said.

"I have named it Nammu," said Quinn. "When it is around, our luck has held."

Zain stared out into the never-ending waves.

"Let us hope that you are right," he said. "I think the next part of our journey will prove even trickier than the first."

"If Nammu is with us, good fortune is with us," said Quinn, with more confidence than he felt. He thought back on all that they had experienced in the four months since leaving home – storms, monsters, dragons, capture (first by the strange tribe, then by the Gelynions), robbery, betrayal, ice, snow, injury – and Zain thought things were going to get worse . . .

Nammu or no Nammu, confident words aside, deep down in the folds of his warm cloak, where no one could see, Quinn crossed his fingers.

Collect the Whole Series

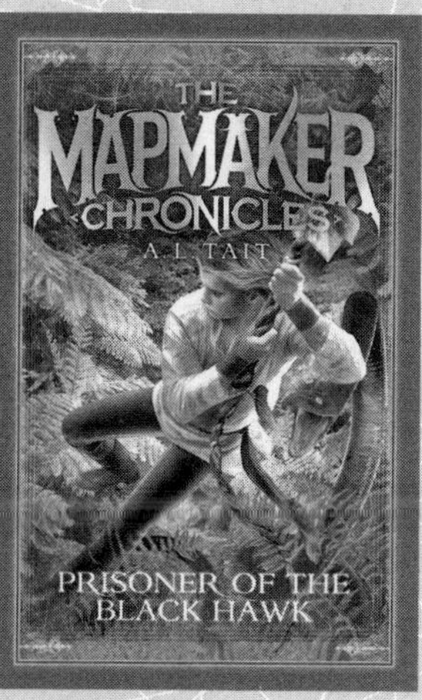

Acknowledgments

This story is a work of fiction, set in a mythical, made-up world, but the mapmaking techniques that Quinn uses are loosely based on the navigation feats of those early brave sailors and explorers who first decided that there was more to the world than what they knew – and set out to discover it. We all owe them a great deal.

In bringing the story to you, I owe so much to my world-beating agent Sophie Hamley, and the intrepid team at Hachette Australia, particularly Suzanne O'Sullivan, Kate Stevens, Chris Kunz, Ashleigh Barton, Fiona Hazard and Matt Richell, as well as cover designers Blacksheep.

Every writer needs a team, and mine is large in number and big on enthusiasm.

To my family, Bev, Dennis, Bronwyn, Christine and Michael, thanks for being the world's greatest cheerleaders.

To my support crew (in alphabetical order) – Alex Brooks, Mark Dapin, Kelly Exeter, Lisa Heidke,

Valerie Khoo, Allison Rushby, Kerri Sackville and Anna Spargo-Ryan – thanks for talking me down from the ceiling when required.

Thank you to my Pink Fibro community – there's nothing quite like being able to go online at any time of the day or night and find someone willing to offer encouragement.

And thank you to all my friends for asking, "Where's the book?" on a regular basis and keeping me on track.

Saving the best for last, thanks and love, to my boys: John, Joseph and Lucas. I couldn't do it without you.

A. L. Tait, who writes fiction and nonfiction for adults under another name, grew up dreaming of world domination. Unfortunately, at the time there were only alphabet sisters B. L. and C. A. and long-suffering brother M. D. M. to practice on . . . and parents who didn't look kindly upon sword fights, plank walking or thumbscrews. But dreams don't die and The Mapmaker Chronicles, the author's first series of books for children, is the result.

A. L. Tait lives in country NSW, Australia, with a family, a garden and four goldfish.